JOHN UPDIKE

a winner of the 1964 National Book Award for his novel *The Centaur*, has been hailed by the critics as "the most gifted writer of his generation" for his novels and short stories.

Updike studied at Harvard College and the Ruskin School of Drawing and Fine Art at Oxford. He has written novels, short stories, poems, essays, and a play. His works include *Rabbit, Run; Rabbit Redux; Couples;* and *Marry Me,* all available in Fawcett Crest paperback editions.

Fawcett Crest and Premier Books
by John Updike:

THE POORHOUSE FAIR
RABBIT, RUN
PIGEON FEATHERS
THE CENTAUR
OF THE FARM
THE MUSIC SCHOOL
COUPLES
RABBIT REDUX
A MONTH OF SUNDAYS
PICKED-UP PIECES
MARRY ME
TOO FAR TO GO
THE COUP

John Updike

TOO FAR TO GO

The Maples Stories

FAWCETT CREST • NEW YORK

A Fawcett Crest Book
Published by Ballantine Books

ISBN 0-449-20016-7

This edition published by arrangement with Alfred A. Knopf

Manufactured in the United States of America

First Fawcett Crest Edition: March 1979
First Ballantine Books Edition: April 1982

ACKNOWLEDGMENTS

Nine of these stories first appeared in *The New Yorker*. "Your Lover Just Called," "Eros Rampant," and "Sublimating" were originally published in *Harper's Magazine*; "Waiting Up" in *Weekend*; "The Red-Herring Theory" in *The New York Times Sunday Magazine*; "Nakedness" in *The Atlantic Monthly*; and "Gesturing" in *Playboy*. Seven of the seventeen have not previously been collected in book form.

The quotations concerning science in "Here Come the Maples" are from a talk by Professor Steven Weinberg, "The Forces of Nature," given before the American Academy of Arts and Sciences and reprinted in that organization's January 1976 bulletin.

Contents

Foreword

The Maples presented themselves to the writer in New York City in 1956, dropped from his sight for seven years, and reappeared in the suburbs of Boston in 1963, giving blood. They figured in a dozen stories since, until the couple's divorce in 1976. Their name, bestowed by a young man who had grown up in a small town shaded by Norway maples, and who then moved to the New England of sugar maples and flame-bright swamp maples, retained for him an arboreal innocence, a straightforward and cooling leafiness. Though the Maples stories trace the decline and fall of a marriage, they also illumine a history in many ways happy, of growing children and a million mundane moments shared. That a marriage ends is less than ideal; but all things end under heaven, and if temporality is held to be invalidating, then nothing real succeeds. The moral of these stories is that all blessings are mixed. Also, that people are incorrigibly themselves. The musical pattern, the advance and retreat, of the Maples' duet is repeated over and over, ever more harshly transposed. They are shy, cheerful, and dissatisfied. They like one another, and are mysteries to one another. One of them is usually feeling slightly unwell, and the seesaw of their erotic interest rarely balances. Yet they talk, more easily than any other characters the author has acted as agent for. A tribe segregated in a valley develops an accent, then a dialect, and then a language all its own; so does a couple. Let this collection preserve one particular dead tongue, no easier to parse than Latin. To the fourteen Maples stories I have added two that from the internal evidence appear to take place in Richard Maple's mind, and a fragment that cried off completion.

J. U.

TOO FAR TO GO

Snowing in Greenwich Village

The Maples had moved just the day before to West
Thirteenth Street, and that evening they had Re-
a Cune over, because now they were so close.
always slightly smiling girl with an absent
he allowed Richard Maple to slip off her
rf even as she stood gently greeting
moving with an extra precision and
the smoothness with which the
anaged—though he and Joan
ver a year, he was still so
did not instinctively lay
reluctance worked in

him a corresponding hesitancy, so that often it was his wife who poured the drinks, while he sprawled on the sofa in the attitude of a favored and wholly delightful guest—entered the dark bedroom, entrusted the bed with Rebecca's clothes, and returned to the living room. Her coat had seemed weightless.

Rebecca, seated beneath the lamp, on the floor, one leg tucked under her, one arm up on the Hide-a-Bed that the previous tenants had not as yet removed, was saying, "I had known her, you know, just for the day she taught me the job, but I said O.K. I was living in an awful place called a hotel for ladies. In the halls they had typewriters you put a quarter in."

Joan, straight-backed on a Hitchcock chair from her parents' home in Vermont, a damp handkerchief balled in her hand, turned to Richard and explained, "Before her apartment now, Becky lived with this girl and her boy friend."

"Yes, his name was Jacques," Rebecca said.

Richard asked, "You lived with them?" The ar
composure of his tone was left over from the m
aroused in him by his successful and, in the
bedroom, somewhat poignant disposal of
guest's coat.

"Yes, and he insisted on having his n
the mailbox. He was terribly afraid of r
letter. When my brother was in the Navy

to see me and saw on the mailbox"—with three parallel movements of her fingers she set the names beneath one another—

"Georgene Clyde,
Rebecca Cune,
Jacques Zimmerman,

he told me I had always been such a nice girl. Jacques wouldn't even move out so my brother would have a place to sleep. He had to sleep on the floor." She lowered her lids and looked in her purse for a cigarette.

"Isn't that wonderful?" Joan said, her smile broadening helplessly as she realized what an inane thing it had been to say. Her cold worried Richard. It had lasted a full week without improving. Her face was pale, mottled pink and yellow; this accentuated the Modiglianiesque quality established by her long neck and oval blue eyes and her habit of sitting to her full height, her head quizzically tilted and her hands palm downward in her lap.

Rebecca, too, was pale, but in the consistent way of a drawing, perhaps—the weight of her lids and a certain virtuosity about the mouth suggested it—by da Vinci.

"Who would like some sherry?" Richard asked in a deep voice, from a standing position.

"We have some hard stuff if you'd rather," Joan said to Rebecca; from Richard's viewpoint the remark, like those advertisements which from varying angles read differently, contained the quite legible declaration that this time *he* would have to mix the drinks.

"The sherry sounds fine," Rebecca said. She enunciated her words distinctly, but in a faint, thin voice that disclaimed for them any consequence.

"I think, too," Joan said.

"Good." So all could share in the drama of it, Richard uncorked the bottle of Tio Pepe in the living room. He posingly poured out three glasses, passed them around, and leaned against the mantel (the Maples had never had a mantel before) until his wife said, as she always did, it being the standard toast in her parents' home, "Cheers, dears!"

Rebecca continued the story of her first apartment. Jacques had never worked. Georgene never held a job more than three weeks. The three of them contributed to a kitty, to which all enjoyed equal access. Rebecca had a separate bedroom. Jacques and Georgene sometimes worked on television scripts; they pinned the bulk of their hopes onto a serial titled *The IBI*—"I" for Intergalactic, or Interplanetary, or something—*in Space and Time*. One of their friends was a young Communist who never washed and always had money because his father owned half of the West Side. During the day, when the two girls were off working, Jacques flirted with a young Swede upstairs who kept dropping her mop onto the tiny balcony outside their window. "A real bombardier," Rebecca said. When Rebecca moved into a single apartment for herself and was all settled and happy, Georgene and Jacques offered to bring a mattress and sleep on her floor. Rebecca felt that the time had come for her to put her foot down. She said no. Later, Jacques married a girl other than Georgene.

"Cashews, anybody?" Richard said. He had bought a can at the corner delicatessen, expressly for this visit, though if Rebecca had not been coming, he would have bought something else there on some other excuse, just for the pleasure of buying his first thing at the store where in the coming years he would purchase so much.

"No thank you," Rebecca said. Richard was so far from expecting refusal that out of momentum he pressed them on her again, exclaiming, "Please! They're so good for you." She took two and bit one in half.

He offered the dish—a silver porringer given to the Maples as a wedding present and until yesterday, for lack of space, never unpacked—to his wife, who took a greedy handful and looked so pale that he asked, "How do you feel?"—not so much forgetting the presence of their guest as parading his concern, quite genuine at that, before her.

"Fine," Joan said edgily, and perhaps she did.

Though the Maples told some stories—how they had lived in a log cabin at a camp on an island in Lake Winnipesaukee for the first three months of their married life, how the whistle on the mail boat taking them there had deafened them for days, how Bitsy Flaner, a mutual friend, was the only girl enrolled in Bentham Divinity School, how Richard's company was thinking of opening a Boston office—they did not regard themselves (that is, each other) as raconteurs, and Rebecca's slight voice dominated the talk. She had a gift for odd things.

Her rich uncle lived in a metal house, furnished with auditorium chairs. He was terribly afraid of fire. Right before the depression he had built an enormous boat to take himself and some friends to Polynesia. All his friends lost their money in the crash. He did not. He made money. He made money out of everything. But he couldn't go on the trip alone, so the boat was still waiting in Oyster Bay, a huge thing rising thirty feet out of water. The uncle was a vegetarian. Rebecca had not eaten turkey for Thanksgiving until she was thirteen years old because it was the family custom to go to the uncle's house on that holiday. The custom was dropped during the war, when the children's synthetic heels made black marks all over his asbestos floor. Rebecca's family had not spoken to the uncle since. "Yes, what got me," Rebecca said, "was the way each new wave of vegetables would come in as if it were a different course."

Richard poured the sherry around again and, because this made him the center of attention anyway, said, "Don't some vegetarians have turkeys molded out of crushed nuts for Thanksgiving?"

After a stretch of silence, Joan said, "I don't know." Her voice, unused for ten minutes, cracked on the last syllable. She cleared her throat, scraping Richard's heart.

"What would they stuff them with?" Rebecca asked, dropping an ash into the saucer beside her.

Beyond and beneath the windows there arose a clatter. Joan reached the windows first, Richard next, and lastly Rebecca, standing on tiptoe, elongating her neck. Six mounted police, standing in their stirrups, were galloping two abreast down Thirteenth Street. When the Maples' exclamations had subsided, Rebecca remarked, "They do it every night at this time. They seem awfully jolly, for policemen."

"Oh, and it's snowing!" Joan cried. She was pathetic about snow; she loved it so much, and in these last years had seen so little. "On our first night here! Our first *real* night." Forgetting herself, she put her arms around Richard, and Rebecca, where another guest might have turned away, or smiled too broadly, too encouragingly, retained without modification her sweet, absent look and studied, through the embracing couple, the scene outdoors. The snow was not taking on the wet street; only the hoods and tops of parked automobiles showed an accumulation.

"I think I'd best go," Rebecca said.

"Please don't," Joan said with an urgency Richard had not expected; clearly she was very tired. Probably the new home, the change in the weather, the good sherry, the currents of affection between herself and her husband that her sudden hug had renewed, and Rebecca's presence had become in her mind the inextricable elements of one enchanting moment.

"Yes, I think I'll go because you're so snuffly and peakèd."

"Can't you just stay for one more cigarette? Dick, pass the sherry around."

"A teeny bit," Rebecca said, holding out her glass. "I guess I told you, Joan, about the boy I went out with who pretended to be a headwaiter."

Joan giggled expectantly. "No, honestly, you never did." She hooked her arm over the back of the chair and wound her hand through the slats, like a child assuring herself that her bedtime has been postponed. "What did he do? He imitated headwaiters?"

"Yes, he was the kind of guy who, when we get out of a taxi and there's a grate giving out steam, crouches down"—Rebecca lowered her head and lifted her arms—"and pretends he's the Devil."

The Maples laughed, less at the words themselves than at the way Rebecca had evoked the situation by conveying, in her understated imitation, both her escort's flamboyant attitude and her own undemonstrative nature. They could see her standing by the taxi door, gazing with no expression as her escort bent lower and lower, seized by his own joke, his fingers writhing demoniacally as he felt horns sprout through his scalp, flames lick his ankles, and his feet shrivel into hoofs. Rebecca's gift, Richard realized, was not that of having odd things happen to her but that of representing, through the implicit contrast with her own sane calm, all things touching her as odd. This evening too might appear grotesque in her retelling: "Six policemen on horses galloped by and she cried 'It's snowing!' and hugged him. He kept telling her how sick she was and filling us full of sherry."

"What else did he do?" Joan asked.

"At the first place we went to—it was a big night club on the roof of somewhere—on the way out he sat down and played the piano until a woman at a harp asked him to stop."

Richard asked, "Was the woman *playing* the harp?"

"Yes, she was strumming away." Rebecca made circular motions with her hands.

"Well, did he play the tune she was playing? Did he *accompany* her?" Petulance, Richard realized without understanding why, had entered his tone.

"No, he just sat down and played something else. I couldn't tell what it was."

"Is this *really* true?" Joan asked, egging her on.

"And then at the next place we went to, we had to wait at the bar for a table and I looked around and he was walking among the tables asking people if everything was all right."

"Wasn't it *aw*ful?" asked Joan.

"Yes. Later he played the piano there, too. We were sort of the main attraction. Around midnight he thought we ought to go out to Brooklyn to his sister's house. I was exhausted. We got off the subway two stops too early, under the Manhattan Bridge. It was deserted, with nothing going by except black limousines. Miles above our head"—she stared up, as though at a cloud, or the sun—"was the Manhattan Bridge and he kept saying it was the el. We finally found some steps and two policemen who told us to go back to the subway."

"What does this amazing man do for a living?" Richard asked.

"He teaches school. He's quite bright." She stood up, extending in stretch a long, silvery white arm. Richard got her coat and said he'd walk her home.

"It's only three-quarters of a block," Rebecca protested in a voice free of any insistent inflection.

"You must walk her home, Dick," Joan said. "Pick up a pack of cigarettes." The idea of his walking in the snow seemed to please her, as if she were anticipating how he would bring back with him, in the snow on his shoulders and the coldness of his face, all the sensations of the walk she was not well enough to risk.

"You should stop smoking for a day or two," he told her.

Joan waved them goodbye from the head of the stairs.

The snow, invisible except around street lights, exerted a fluttering romantic pressure on their faces. "Coming down hard now," he said.

"Yes."

At the corner, where the snow gave the green light a watery blueness, her hesitancy in following him as he turned to walk with the light across

Thirteenth Street led him to ask, "It *is* this side of the street you live on, isn't it?"

"Yes."

"I thought I remembered from the time we drove you down from Boston." The Maples had lived in the West Eighties then. "I remember I had an impression of big buildings."

"The church and the butchers' school," Rebecca said. "Every day about ten when I'm going to work the boys learning to be butchers come out for an intermission all bloody and laughing."

Richard looked up at the church; the steeple was fragmentarily silhouetted against the scattered lit windows of a tall improvement on Seventh Avenue. "Poor church," he said. "It's hard in this city for a steeple to be the tallest thing."

Rebecca said nothing, not even her habitual "Yes." He felt rebuked for being preachy. In his embarrassment he directed her attention to the first next thing he saw, a poorly lettered sign above a great door. "Food Trades Vocational High School," he read aloud. "The people upstairs told us that the man before the man before *us* in our apartment was a wholesale meat salesman who called himself a Purveyor of Elegant Foods. He kept a woman in the apartment."

"Those big windows up there," Rebecca said, pointing up at the third story of a brownstone, "face mine across the street. I can look in and feel we are neighbors. Someone's always in there; I don't know what they do for a living."

After a few more steps they halted, and Rebecca, in a voice that Richard imagined to be slightly louder than her ordinary one, said, "Do you want to come up and see where I live?"

"Sure." It seemed implausible to refuse.

They descended four concrete steps, opened a shabby orange door, entered an overheated half-basement lobby, and began to climb three flights of wooden stairs. Richard's suspicion on the street that he was trespassing beyond the public gardens of courtesy turned to certain guilt. Few experiences so savor of the illicit as mounting stairs behind a woman's fanny. Three years ago, Joan had lived in a fourth-floor walk-up, in Cambridge. Richard never took her home, even when the whole business, down to the last intimacy, had become formula, without the fear that the landlord, justifiably furious, would leap from his door and devour him as they passed.

Opening her door, Rebecca said, "It's hot as hell in here," swearing for the first time in his hearing. She turned on a weak light. The room was small; slanting planes, the underside of the building's roof, intersecting the ceiling and walls, cut large prismatic volumes from Rebecca's living space. As he moved further forward, toward Rebecca, who had not yet removed her coat, Richard perceived, on his right, an unexpected area created where the steeply slanting roof extended itself to the floor. Here a double bed was placed. Tightly bounded on three sides, the bed had the appearance not so much of a piece of furniture as of a permanently installed, blanketed platform. He quickly took his eyes from it and, unable to face Rebecca at once, stared at two kitchen chairs, a metal bridge lamp around the rim of whose shade plump fish and helm wheels alternated, and a plank-and-brick bookcase—all of which, being proximate to a tilting wall, had an air of threatened verticality.

"Yes, here's the stove on top of the refrigerator I told you about," Rebecca said. "Or did I?"

The top unit overhung the lower by several inches on all sides. He touched his fingers to the stove's white side. "This room is quite sort of nice," he said.

"Here's the view," she said. He moved to stand beside her at the windows, lifting aside the curtains and peering through tiny flawed panes into the apartment across the street.

"That guy *does* have a huge window," Richard said.

She made a brief agreeing noise of *n*'s.

Though all the lamps were on, the apartment across the street was empty. "Looks like a furniture store," he said. Rebecca had still not taken off her coat. "The snow's keeping up."

"Yes. It is."

"Well"—this word was too loud; he finished the sentence too softly—"thanks for letting me see it. I—have you read this?" He had noticed a copy of *Auntie Mame* lying on a hassock.

"I haven't had the time," she said.

"I haven't read it either. Just reviews. That's all I ever read."

This got him to the door. There, ridiculously, he turned. It was only at the door, he decided in retrospect, that her conduct was hard to explain: not only did she stand unnecessarily close, but, by shifting the weight of her body to one leg and leaning her head sideways, she lowered her height several inches, placing him in a dominating position exactly fitted to the broad, passive shadows she must have known were on her face.

"Well . . ." he said.

"Well." Her echo was immediate and possibly meaningless.

"Don't, don't let the b-butchers get you." The stammer of course ruined the joke, and her laugh, which had begun as soon as she had seen by his face that he would attempt something funny, was completed ahead of his utterance.

As he went down the stairs she rested both hands

on the banister and looked down toward the next landing. "Goodnight," she said.

"Night." He looked up; she had gone into her room. Oh but they were close.

Wife-wooing

Oh my love. Yes. Here we sit, on warm broad floorboards, before a fire, the children between us, in a crescent, eating. The girl and I share one half-pint of French-fried potatoes; you and the boy share another; and in the center, sharing nothing, making simple reflections within himself like a jewel, the baby, mounted in an Easybaby, sucks at his bottle with frowning mastery, his selfish, contemplative eyes stealing glitter from the center of the flames. And you. You. You allow your skirt, the same black skirt in which this morning you with woman's soft bravery mounted a bicycle and sallied forth to play hymns in difficult keys on the Sunday school's old piano—you allow this black skirt to slide off your raised knees down your thighs, slide *up* your thighs in your body's absolute geography, so the parallel whiteness of their undersides is exposed to the fire's warmth and to my sight. Oh. There is a line of Joyce. I try to recover it from the legendary, imperfectly explored grottoes of *Ulysses:* a garter snapped, to please Blazes Boylan, in a deep Dublin den. What? Smackwarm. That was the crucial word. Smacked smackwarm on her smackable warm woman's thigh. Something like that. A splendid man, to feel that. Smackwarm woman's. Splendid also to feel the curious and potent, inexplicable and irrefutably magical life language leads within itself. What soul took thought and knew that adding "wo" to man would make a woman? The difference exactly. The wide w, the receptive o. Womb. In our crescent the children for all their size seem to come out of you toward me, wet fingers and eyes, tinted bronze. Three children, five persons, seven years. Seven years since I wed wide warm woman, white-thighed. Wooed and wed. Wife. A knife of a word that for all its final bite did not end the wooing. To my wonderment.

We eat meat, meat I wrestled warm from the raw hands of the hamburger girl in the diner a mile away, a ferocious place, slick with savagery, wild with chrome; young predators snarling dirty jokes menaced me, old men reached for me with coffee-warmed paws; I wielded my wallet, and won my way back. The fat brown bag of buns was warm beside me in the cold car; the smaller bag holding the two tiny cartons of French-fries emitted an even more urgent heat. Back through the black winter air to the fire, the intimate cave, where halloos and hurrahs greeted me, the deer, mouth agape and its cotton throat gushing, stretched dead across my shoulders. And now you, beside the white O of the plate upon which the children discarded with squeals of disgust the rings of translucent onion that came squeezed into the hamburgers—you push your toes an inch closer to the blaze, and the ashy white of the inside of your deep thigh is lazily laid bare, and the eternally elastic garter snaps smack-warm against my hidden heart.

Who would have thought, wide wife, back there in the white tremble of the ceremony (in the corner of my eye I held, despite the distracting hail of ominous vows, the vibration of the cluster of stephanotis clutched against your waist), that seven years would bring us no distance, through all those warm beds, to the same trembling point, of beginning? The cells change every seven years and down in the atom, apparently, there is a strange discontinuity; as if God wills the universe anew every instant. (Ah God, dear God, tall friend of my childhood, I will never forget you, though they say dreadful things. They say rose windows in cathedrals are vaginal symbols.) Your legs, exposed as fully as by a bathing suit, yearn deeper into the amber wash of heat. Well: begin. A green jet of flame spits out sideways from a pocket of resin in a log, crying, and the orange shadows on the ceiling sway with fresh life. Begin.

"Remember, on our honeymoon, how the top of the kerosene heater made a great big rose window on the ceiling?"

"Vnn." Your chin goes to your knees, your shins draw in, all is retracted. Not much to remember, perhaps, for you; blood badly spilled, clumsiness of all sorts. "It was cold for June."

"Mommy, what was cold? What did you say?" the girl asks, enunciating angrily, determined not to let language slip on her tongue and tumble her so that we laugh.

"A house where Daddy and I stayed one time."

"I don't like dat," the boy says, and throws a half bun painted with chartreuse mustard onto the floor.

You pick it up and with beautiful somber musing ask, "Isn't that funny? Did any of the others have mustard on them?"

"I *hate* dat," the boy insists; he is two. Language

is to him thick vague handles swirling by; he grabs what he can.

"Here. He can have mine. Give me his." I pass my hamburger over, you take it, he takes it from you, there is nowhere a ripple of gratitude. There is no more praise of my heroism in fetching Sunday supper, saving you labor. Cunning, you sense, and sense that I sense your knowledge, that I had hoped to hoard your energy toward a more ecstatic spending. We sense everything between us, every ripple, existent and nonexistent; it is tiring. Courting a wife takes tenfold the strength of winning an ignorant girl. The fire shifts, shattering fragments of newspaper that carry in lighter gray the ghost of the ink of their message. You huddle your legs and bring the skirt back over them. With a sizzling noise like the sighs of the exhausted logs, the baby sucks the last from his bottle, drops it to the floor with its distasteful hoax of vacant suds, and begins to cry. His egotist's mouth opens; the delicate membrane of his satisfaction tears. You pick him up and stand. You love the baby more than me.

Who would have thought, blood once spilled, that no barrier would be broken, that you would be each time healed into a virgin again? Tall, fair, obscure, remote, and courteous.

We put the children to bed, one by one, in reverse order of birth. I am limitlessly patient, paternal, good. Yet you know. We watch the paper bags and cartons ignite on the breathing pillow of embers, read, watch television, eat crackers, it does not matter. Eleven comes. For a tingling moment you stand on the bedroom rug in your underpants, untangling your nightie; oh, fat white sweet fat fatness. In bed you read. About Richard Nixon. He fascinates you; you hate him. You know how he defeated Jerry Voorhis, martyred Mrs. Douglas, how he played poker in the Navy despite being a Quaker, every fiendish trick, every low adaptation. Oh my Lord. Let's let the poor man go to bed. We're none of us perfect. "Hey, let's turn out the light."

"Wait. He's just about to get Hiss convicted. It's very strange. It says he acted honorably."

"I'm sure he did." I reach for the switch.

"No. Wait. Just till I finish this chapter. I'm sure there'll be something at the end."

"Honey, Hiss was guilty. We're all guilty. Conceived in concupiscence, we die unrepentant." Once my ornate words wooed you.

I lie against your filmy convex back. You read sideways, a sleepy trick. I see the page through the fringe of your hair, sharp and white as a wedge of crystal. Suddenly it slips. The book has slipped from your hand. You are asleep. Oh cunning trick, cunning. In the darkness I consider. Cunning. The headlights of cars accidentally slide fanning slits of light around our walls and ceiling. The great rose window was projected upward through the petal-shaped perforations in the top of the black kerosene stove, which we stood in the center of the floor. As the flame on the circular wick flickered, the wide soft star of interlocked penumbrae moved and waved as if it were printed on a silk cloth being gently tugged or slowly blown. Its color soft blurred blood. We pay dear in blood for our peaceful homes.

In the morning, to my relief, you are ugly. Monday's wan breakfast light bleaches you blotchily, drains the goodness from your thickness, makes the bathrobe a limp stained tube flapping disconsolately, exposing sallow décolletage. The skin between your breasts a sad yellow. I feast with the coffee on your drabness. Every wrinkle and sickly tint a relief and a revenge. The children yammer. The toaster sticks. Seven years have worn this woman.

The man, he arrows off to work, jousting for right-of-way, veering on the thin hard edge of the legal speed limit. Out of domestic muddle, softness, pallor, flaccidity: into the city. Stone is his province. The winning of coin. The maneuvering of abstractions. Making heartless things run. Oh the inanimate, adamant joys of job!

I return with my head enmeshed in a machine. A technicality it would take weeks to explain to you snags my brain; I fiddle with phrases and numbers all the blind evening. You serve me supper as a waitress—as less than a waitress, for I have known you. The children touch me timidly, as they would a steep girder bolted into a framework whose height they don't understand. They drift into sleep securely. We survive their passing in calm parallelity. My thoughts rework in chronic right angles the same snagging circuits on the same professional grid. You rustle the book about Nixon; vanish upstairs into the plumbing; the bathtub pipes cry. In my head I seem to have found the stuck switch at last: I push at it; it jams; I push; it is jammed. I grow dizzy, churning with cigarettes. I circle the room aimlessly.

So I am taken by surprise at a turning when at the meaningful hour of ten you come with a kiss of toothpaste to me moist and girlish and quick; the momentous moral of this story being, An expected gift is not worth giving.

Giving Blood

The Maples had been married now nine years, which is almost too long. "Goddammit, goddammit," Richard said to Joan, as they drove into Boston to give blood, "I drive this road five days a week and now I'm driving it again. It's like a nightmare. I'm exhausted. I'm emotionally, mentally, physically exhausted, and she isn't even an aunt of mine. She isn't even an aunt of *yours*."

"She's a sort of cousin," Joan said.

"Well hell, every goddam body in New England is some sort of cousin of yours; must I spend the rest of my life trying to save them *all?*"

"Hush," Joan said. "She might die. I'm ashamed of you. Really ashamed."

It cut. His voice for the moment took on an apologetic pallor. "Well I'd be my usual goddam saintly self if I'd had any sort of sleep last night. Five days a week I bump out of bed and stagger out the door past the milkman and on the one day of the week when I don't even have to truck the blasphemous little brats to Sunday school you make an appointment to have me drained dry thirty miles away."

"Well it wasn't *me*," Joan said, "who had to stay till two o'clock doing the Twist with Marlene Brossman."

"We weren't doing the Twist. We were gliding around very chastely to 'Hits of the Forties.' And don't think I was so oblivious I didn't see you snoogling behind the piano with Harry Saxon."

"We weren't behind the piano, we were on the bench. And he was just talking to me because he felt sorry for me. Everybody there felt sorry for me; you could have at *least* let somebody else dance *once* with Marlene, if only for show."

"Show, show," Richard said. "That's your mentality exactly."

"Why, the poor Matthews or whatever they are looked absolutely horrified."

"Matthiessons," he said. "And that's another

thing. Why are idiots like that being invited these days? If there's anything I hate, it's women who keep putting one hand on their pearls and taking a deep breath. I thought she had something stuck in her throat."

"They're a perfectly pleasant, decent young couple. The thing you resent about their coming is that their being there shows us what we've become."

"If you're so attracted," he said, "to little fat men like Harry Saxon, why didn't you marry one?"

"My," Joan said calmly, and gazed out the window away from him, at the scudding gasoline stations. "You honestly *are* hateful. It's not just a pose."

"Pose, show, my Lord, who are you performing for? If it isn't Harry Saxon, it's Freddie Vetter—all these dwarves. Every time I looked over at you last night it was like some pale Queen of the Dew surrounded by a ring of mushrooms."

"You're too absurd," she said. Her hand, distinctly thirtyish, dry and green-veined and rasped by detergents, stubbed out her cigarette in the dashboard ashtray. "You're not subtle. You think you can match me up with another man so you can swirl off with Marlene with a free conscience."

Her reading his strategy so correctly made his face burn; he felt again the tingle of Mrs. Brossman's hair as he pressed his cheek against hers and in this damp privacy inhaled the perfume behind her ear. "You're right," he said. "But I want to get you a man your own size; I'm very loyal that way."

"Let's not talk," she said.

His hope, of turning the truth into a joke, was rebuked. Any implication of permission was blocked. "It's that *smug*ness," he explained, speaking levelly, as if about a phenomenon of which they were both disinterested students. "It's your smugness that is really intolerable. Your stupidity I don't mind. Your sexlessness I've learned to live with. But that wonderfully smug, New England—I suppose we needed it to get the country founded, but in the Age of Anxiety it really does gall."

He had been looking over at her, and unexpectedly she turned and looked at him, with a startled but uncannily crystalline expression, as if her face had been in an instant rendered in tinted porcelain, even to the eyelashes.

"I asked you not to talk," she said. "Now you've said things that I'll always remember."

Plunged fathoms deep into the wrong, his face suffocated with warmth, he concentrated on the highway and sullenly steered. Though they were moving at sixty in the sparse Saturday traffic, he had traveled this road so often its distances were all translated into time, so that they seemed to him to be moving as slowly as a minute hand from one digit to the next. It would have been strategic and dignified of him to keep the silence; but he could not resist believing that just one more pinch of syllables would restore the fine balance which with each wordless mile slipped increasingly awry. He asked, "How did Bean seem to you?" Bean was their baby. They had left her last night, to go to the party, with a fever of 102.

Joan wrestled with her vow to say nothing, but guilt proved stronger than spite. She said, "Cooler. Her nose is a river."

"Sweetie," Richard blurted, "will they hurt me?" The curious fact was that he had never given blood before. Asthmatic and underweight, he had been 4-F, and at college and now at the office he had, less through his own determination than through the diffidence of the solicitors, evaded pledging blood. It was one of those tests of courage so trivial that no one had ever thought to make him face up to it.

Spring comes carefully to Boston. Speckled crusts of ice lingered around the parking meters, and the air, grayly stalemated between seasons, tinted the buildings along Longwood Avenue with a drab and homogeneous majesty. As they walked up the drive to the hospital entrance, Richard nervously wondered aloud if they would see the King of Arabia.

"He's in a separate wing," Joan said. "With four wives."

"Only four? What an ascetic." And he made bold to tap his wife's shoulder. It was not clear if, under the thickness of her winter coat, she felt it.

At the desk, they were directed down a long corridor floored with cigar-colored linoleum. Up and down, right and left it went, in the secretive, disjointed way peculiar to hospitals that have been built annex by annex. Richard seemed to himself Hansel orphaned with Gretel; birds ate the bread crumbs behind them, and at last they timidly knocked on the witch's door, which said BLOOD DONATION CENTER. A young man in white opened the door a crack. Over his shoulder Richard glimpsed—horrors!—a pair of dismembered female legs stripped of their shoes and laid parallel on a bed. Glints of needles and bottles pricked his eyes. Without widening the crack, the young man passed out to them two long forms. In sitting side by side on the waiting bench, remembering their middle initials and childhood diseases, Mr. and Mrs. Maple were newly defined to themselves. He fought down that urge to giggle and clown and lie that threatened him whenever he was asked—like a lawyer appointed by the court to plead a hopeless case—to present, as it were, his statistics to eternity. It seemed to mitigate his case slightly that a few of these statistics (present address, date of marriage) were shared by the hurt soul scratching beside him, with his own pen. He looked over her shoulder. "I never knew you had whooping cough."

"My mother says. I don't remember it."

A pan crashed to a distant floor. An elevator chuckled remotely. A woman, a middle-aged woman top-heavy with rouge and fur, stepped out of the blood door and wobbled a moment on legs that looked familiar. They had been restored to their shoes. The heels of these shoes clicked firmly as, having raked the Maples with a defiant blue glance, she turned and disappeared around a bend in the corridor. The young man appeared in the doorway holding a pair of surgical tongs. His noticeably recent haircut made him seem an apprentice barber. He clicked his tongs and smiled. "Shall I do you together?"

"Sure." It put Richard on his mettle that this callow fellow, to whom apparently they were to entrust their liquid essence, was so clearly younger than they. But when Richard stood, his indignation melted and his legs felt diluted under him. And the extraction of the blood sample from his middle finger seemed the nastiest and most needlessly prolonged physical involvement with another human being he had ever experienced. There is a touch that good dentists, mechanics, and barbers have, and this intern did not have it; he fumbled and in compensation was too rough. Again and again, an atrociously clumsy vampire, he tugged and twisted the purpling finger in vain. The tiny glass capillary tube remained transparent.

"He doesn't like to bleed, does he?" the intern asked Joan. As relaxed as a nurse, she sat in a chair next to a table of scintillating equipment.

"I don't think his blood moves much," she said, "until after midnight."

This stab at a joke made Richard in his extremity of fright laugh loudly, and the laugh at last seemed to jar the panicked coagulant. Red seeped upward in the thirsty little tube, as in a sudden thermometer.

The intern grunted in relief. As he smeared the samples on the analysis box, he explained idly, "What we ought to have down here is a pan of warm water. You just came in out of the cold. If you put your hand in hot water for a minute, the blood just pops out."

"A pretty thought," Richard said.

But the intern had already written him off as a clowner and continued calmly to Joan, "All we'd need would be a baby hot plate for about six dollars, then we could make our own coffee too. This way, when we get a donor who needs the coffee afterward, we have to send up for it while we keep his head between his knees. Do you think you'll be needing coffee?"

"No," Richard interrupted, jealous of their rapport.

The intern told Joan, "You're O."

"I know," she said.

"And he's A positive."

"Why that's very good, Dick!" she called to him.

"Am I rare?" he asked.

The boy turned and explained, "O positive and A positive are the most common types." Something in the patient tilt of his close-cropped head as its lateral sheen mixed with the almost-bright midmorning air of the room sharply reminded Richard of the days years ago when he had tended a battery of Teletype machines in a room much this size. By now, ten o'clock, the yards of copy that began pouring through the machines at five and that lay in great crimped heaps on the floor when he arrived at seven would have been harvested and sorted and pasted together and turned in, and there was nothing to do but keep up with the staccato appearance of the later news and to think about simple things like coffee. It came back to him, how pleasant and secure those hours had been when, king of his own corner, he was young and newly responsible.

The intern asked, "Who wants to be first?"

"Let me," Joan said. "He's never done it before."

"Her full name is Joan of Arc," Richard explained, angered at this betrayal, so unimpeachably selfless and smug.

The intern, threatened in his element, fixed his puzzled eyes on the floor between them and said, "Take off your shoes and each get on a bed." He added, "Please," and all three laughed, one after the other, the intern last.

The beds were at right angles to one another along two walls. Joan lay down and from her husband's angle of vision was novelly foreshortened. He had never before seen her quite this way, the combed crown of her hair so poignant, her bared arm so silver and long, her stocking feet toed in so childishly and docilely. There were no pillows on the beds, and lying flat made him feel tipped head down; the illusion of floating encouraged his hope that this unreal adventure would soon dissolve in the manner of a dream. "You O.K.?"

"Are you?" Her voice came softly from the tucked-under wealth of her hair. From the straightness of the parting it seemed her mother had brushed it. He watched a long needle sink into the flat of her arm and a piece of moist cotton clumsily swab the spot. He had imagined their blood would be drained into cans or bottles, but the intern, whose breathing was now the only sound within the room, brought to Joan's side what looked like a miniature plastic knapsack, all coiled and tied. His body cloaked his actions. When he stepped away, a plastic cord had been grafted, a transparent vine, to the flattened crook of Joan's extended arm, where the skin was translucent and the veins were faint blue tributaries shallowly buried. It was a tender, vulnerable place where in courting days she had liked being stroked. Now, without visible transition, the pale tendril planted here went dark red. Richard wanted to cry out.

The instant readiness of her blood to leave her body pierced him like a physical pang. Though he had not so much as blinked, its initial leap had been too quick for his eye. He had expected some visible sign of flow, but from the mere appearance of it the tiny looped hose might be pouring blood *into* her body or might be a curved line added, irrelevant as a mustache, to a finished canvas. The fixed position of his head gave what he saw a certain flatness.

And now the intern turned to him, and there was the tiny felt prick of the novocaine needle, and then the coarse, half-felt intrusion of something resembling a medium-weight nail. Twice the boy mistakenly probed for the vein and the third time taped the successful graft fast with adhesive tape. All the while, Richard's mind moved aloofly among the constellations of the stained cracked ceiling.

What was being done to him did not bear contemplating. When the intern moved away to hum and tinkle among his instruments, Joan craned her neck to show her husband her face and, upside down in his vision, grotesquely smiled.

It was not many minutes that they lay there at right angles together, but the time passed as something beyond the walls, as something mixed with the faraway clatter of pans and the approach and retreat of footsteps and the opening and closing of unseen doors. Here, conscious of a pointed painless pulse in the inner hinge of his arm but incurious as to what it looked like, he floated and imagined how his soul would float free when all his blood was underneath the bed. His blood and Joan's merged on the floor, and together their spirits glided from crack to crack, from star to star on the ceiling. Once she cleared her throat, and the sound made an abrasion like the rasp of a pebble loosened by a cliff climber's boot.

The door opened. Richard turned his head and saw an old man, bald and sallow, enter and settle in a chair. He was one of those old men who hold within an institution an ill-defined but consecrated place. The young doctor seemed to know him, and the two talked, softly, as if not to disturb the mystical union of the couple sacrificially bedded together. They talked of persons and events that meant nothing—of Iris, of Dr. Greenstein, of Ward D, again of Iris, who had given the old man an undeserved scolding, of the shameful lack of a hot plate to make coffee on, of the rumored black bodyguards who kept watch with scimitars by the bed of the glaucomatous king. Through Richard's tranced ignorance these topics passed as clouds of impressions, iridescent, massy—Dr. Greenstein with a pointed nose and almond eyes the color of ivy, Iris eighty feet tall and hurling sterilized thunderbolts of wrath. As in some theologies the proliferant deities are said to exist as ripples upon the featureless ground of Godhead, so these inconstant images lightly overlay his continuous awareness of Joan's blood, like his own, ebbing. Linked to a common loss, they were chastely conjoined; the thesis developed upon him that the hoses attached to them somewhere out of sight met. Testing this belief, he glanced down and saw that indeed the plastic vine taped to the flattened crook of his arm was the same dark red as hers. He stared at the ceiling to disperse a sensation of faintness.

Abruptly the young intern left off his desultory conversation and moved to Joan's side. There was a chirp of clips. When he moved away, she was revealed holding her naked arm upright, pressing a piece of cotton against it with the other hand. Without pausing, the intern came to Richard's side, and the birdsong of clips repeated, nearer. "Look at that," he said to his elderly friend. "I started him two minutes later than her and he's finished at the same time."

"Was it a race?" Richard asked.

Clumsily firm, the boy fitted Richard's fingers to a pad and lifted his arm for him. "Hold it there for five minutes," he said.

"What'll happen if I don't?"

"You'll mess up your shirt." To the old man he said, "I had a woman in here the other day, she was all set to leave when all of a sudden, pow!—all over the front of this beautiful linen dress. She was going to Symphony."

"Then they try to sue the hospital for the cleaning bill," the old man muttered.

"Why was I slower than him?" Joan asked. Her upright arm wavered, as if vexed or weakened.

"The woman generally is," the boy told her. "Nine times out of ten, the man is faster. Their hearts are so much stronger."

"Is that really so?"

"Sure it's so," Richard told her. "Don't argue with medical science."

"Woman up in Ward C," the old man said, "they

saved her life for her out of an auto accident and now I hear she's suing because they didn't find her dental plate."

Under such patter, the five minutes eroded. Richard's upheld arm began to ache. It seemed that he and Joan were caught together in a classroom where they would never be recognized, or in a charade that would never be guessed, the correct answer being Two Silver Birches in a Meadow.

"You can sit up now if you want," the intern told them. "But don't let go of the venipuncture."

They sat up on their beds, legs dangling heavily. Joan asked him, "Do you feel dizzy?"

"With my powerful heart? Don't be presumptuous."

"Do you think he'll need coffee?" the intern asked her. "I'll have to send up for it now."

The old man shifted forward in his chair, preparing to heave to his feet.

"I do *not* want any *coffee*"—Richard said it so loud he saw himself transposed, another Iris, into the firmament of the old man's aggrieved gossip. *Some dizzy bastard down in the blood room, I get up to get him some coffee and he damn near bit my head off.* To demonstrate simultaneously his essential good humor and his total presence of mind, Richard gestured toward the blood they had given —two square plastic sacks filled solidly fat—and declared, "Back where I come from in West Virginia sometimes you pick a tick off a dog that looks like that." The men looked at him amazed. Had he not quite said what he meant to say? Or had they never seen anybody from West Virginia before?

Joan pointed at the blood, too. "Is that us? Those little doll pillows?"

"Maybe we should take one home to Bean," Richard suggested.

The intern did not seem convinced that this was a joke. "Your blood will be credited to Mrs. Henryson's account," he stated stiffly.

Joan asked him, "Do you know anything about her? When is she—when is her operation scheduled?"

"I think for tomorrow. The only thing on the tab this after is an open heart or two; that'll take about sixteen pints."

"Oh . . ." Joan was shaken. "Sixteen . . . that's a full person, isn't it?"

"More," the intern answered, with the regal handwave that bestows largess and dismisses compliments.

"Could we visit her?" Richard asked, for Joan's benefit. ("Really ashamed," she had said; it had cut.) He was confident of the refusal.

"Well, you can ask at the desk, but usually before a major one like this it's just the nearest of kin. I guess you're safe now." He meant their punctures. Richard's arm bore a small raised bruise; the intern covered it with one of those ample, salmon, unhesitatingly adhesive bandages that only hospitals have. That was their specialty, Richard thought—packaging. They wrap the human mess for final delivery. Sixteen doll's pillows, uniformly dark and snug, marching into an open heart: the vision momentarily satisfied his hunger for cosmic order.

He rolled down his sleeve and slid off the bed. It startled him to realize, in the instant before his feet touched the floor, that three pairs of eyes were fixed upon him, fascinated and apprehensive and eager for scandal. He stood and towered above them. He hopped on one foot to slip into one loafer, and then on this foot to slip into the other loafer. Then he did the little shuffle-tap, shuffle-tap step that was all that remained to him of dancing lessons he had taken at the age of seven, driving twelve miles each Saturday into Morgantown. He made a small bow toward his wife, smiled at the old man, and said to the intern, "All my life people have been expecting me to faint. I have no idea why. I never faint."

His coat and overcoat felt a shade queer, a bit slithery and light, but as he walked down the length of the corridor, space seemed to adjust snugly around him. At his side, Joan kept an inquisitive and chastened silence. They pushed through the great glass doors. A famished sun was nibbling through the overcast. Above and behind them, the King of Arabia lay in a drugged dream of dunes and Mrs. Henryson upon her sickbed received like the comatose mother of twins their identical gifts of blood. Richard hugged his wife's padded shoulders and as they walked along leaning on each other whispered, "Hey, I love you. Love love *love* you."

Romance is, simply, the strange, the untried. It was unusual for the Maples to be driving together at eleven in the morning. Almost always it was dark when they shared a car. The oval of her face was bright in the corner of his eye. She was watching him, alert to take the wheel if he suddenly lost consciousness. He felt tender toward her in the eggshell light, and curious toward himself, wondering how far beneath his brain the black pit did lie. He felt no different; but then the quality of consciousness perhaps did not bear introspection. Something certainly had been taken from him; he was less himself by a pint and it was not impossible that like a trapeze artist saved by a net he was sustained in the world of light and reflection by a single layer of interwoven cells. Yet the earth, with its signals and buildings and cars and bricks, continued like a pedal note.

Boston behind them, he asked, "Where should we eat?"

"Should we eat?"

"Please, yes. Let me take you to lunch. Just like a secretary."

"I do feel sort of illicit. As if I've stolen something."

"You too? But what did we steal?"

"I don't know. The morning? Do you think Eve knows enough to feed them?" Eve was their sitter, a little sandy girl from down the street who would, in exactly a year, Richard calculated, be painfully lovely. They lasted three years on the average, sitters; you got them in the tenth grade and escorted them into their bloom and then, with graduation, like commuters who had reached their stop, they dropped out of sight, into nursing school or marriage. And the train went on, and took on other passengers, and itself became older and longer. The Maples had four children: Judith, Richard Jr., poor oversized, angel-faced John, and Bean.

"She'll manage. What would you like? All that talk about coffee has made me frantic for some."

"At the Pancake House beyond 128 they give you coffee before you even ask."

"Pancakes? Now? Aren't you gay? Do you think we'll throw up?"

"Do you feel like throwing up?"

"No, not really. I feel sort of insubstantial and gentle, but it's probably psychosomatic. I don't really understand this business of giving something away and still somehow having it. What is it—the spleen?"

"I don't know. Are the splenetic man and the sanguine man the same?"

"God. I've totally forgotten the humors. What are the others—phlegm and choler?"

"Bile and black bile are in there somewhere."

"One thing about you, Joan. You're educated. New England women are educated."

"Sexless as we are."

"That's right; drain me dry and then put me on the rack." But there was no wrath in his words; indeed, he had reminded her of their earlier conversation so that, in much this way, his words might be revived, diluted, and erased. It seemed to work. The restaurant where they served only pancakes was empty and quiet this early. A bashfulness possessed them both; it had become a date between two people who have little as yet in common but who are nevertheless sufficiently intimate to accept the fact without chatter. Touched by the stain her blueberry pancakes left on her teeth, he held a match to her cigarette and said, "Gee, I loved you back in the blood room."

"I wonder why."

"You were so brave."

"So were you."

"But I'm supposed to be. I'm paid to be. It's the price of having a penis."

"Shh."

"Hey, I didn't mean that about your being sexless."

The waitress refilled their coffee cups and gave them the check.

"And I promise never never to do the Twist, the cha-cha, or the schottische with Marlene Brossman."

"Don't be silly. I don't care."

This amounted to permission, but perversely irritated him. That smugness; why didn't she *fight?* Trying to regain their peace, scrambling uphill, he picked up their check and with an effort of acting, the pretense being that they were out on a date and he was a raw dumb suitor, said handsomely, "I'll pay."

But on looking into his wallet he saw only a single worn dollar there. He didn't know why this should make him so angry, except the fact somehow that it was only *one.* "Goddammit," he said. "Look at that." He waved it in her face. "I work like a bastard all week for you and those insatiable brats and at the end of it what do I have? One goddam crummy wrinkled dollar."

Her hands dropped to the pocketbook beside her on the seat, but her gaze stayed with him, her face having retreated, or advanced, into that porcelain shell of uncanny composure. "We'll both pay," Joan said.

Twin Beds in Rome

The Maples had talked and thought about separation so long it seemed it would never come. For their conversations, increasingly ambivalent and ruthless as accusation, retraction, blow, and caress alternated and canceled, had the final effect of knitting them ever tighter together in a painful, helpless, degrading intimacy. And their lovemaking, like a perversely healthy child whose growth defies every deficiency of nutrition, continued; when their tongues at last fell silent, their bodies collapsed together as two mute armies might gratefully mingle, released from the absurd hostilities decreed by two mad kings.

Bleeding, mangled, reverently laid in its tomb a dozen times, their marriage could not die. Burning to leave one another, they left, out of marital habit, together. They took a trip to Rome.

They arrived at night. The plane was late, the airport grand. They had left hastily, without plans; and yet, as if forewarned of their arrival, nimble Italians, speaking perfect English, parted them deftly from their baggage, reserved a hotel room for them by telephone from the airport, and ushered them into a bus. The bus, surprisingly, plunged into a dark rural landscape. A few windows hung lanternlike in the distance; a river abruptly bared its silver breast beneath them; the silhouettes of olive trees and Italian pines flicked past like shadowy illustrations in an old Latin primer. "I could ride this bus forever," Joan said aloud, and Richard was pained, remembering from the days when they had been content together, how she had once confessed to feeling a sexual stir when the young man at the gas station, wiping the windshield with a vigorous, circular motion, had made the body of the car, containing her, rock slightly. Of all the things she had ever told him, this remained in his mind the most revealing, the deepest glimpse she had ever permitted into the secret woman he could never reach and had at last wearied of trying to reach.

Yet it pleased him to have her happy. This was

his weakness. He wished her to be happy, and the certainty that, away from her, he could not know if she were happy or not formed the final, unexpected door barring his way when all others had been opened. So he dried the very tears he had whipped from her eyes, withdrew each protestation of hopelessness at the very point when she seemed willing to give up hope, and their agony continued. "Nothing lasts forever," he said now.

"You can't let me relax a minute, can you?"

"I'm sorry. Do relax."

She stared through the window awhile, then turned and told him, "It doesn't feel as if we're going to Rome at all."

"Where are we going?" He honestly wanted to know, honestly hoped she could tell him.

"Back to the way things were?"

"No. I don't want to go back to that. I feel we've come very far and have only a little way more to go."

She looked out at the quiet landscape a long while before he realized she was crying. He fought the impulse to comfort her, inwardly shouted it down as cowardly and cruel, but his hand, as if robbed of restraint by a force as powerful as lust, crept onto her arm. She rested her head on his shoulder. The shawled woman across the aisle took them for honeymooners and politely glanced away.

The bus slipped from the country. Factories and

residential rows narrowed the highway. A sudden monument, a massive white pyramid stricken with light and inscribed with Latin, loomed beside them. Soon they were pressing their faces together to the window to follow the Colosseum itself as, shaped like a shattered wedding cake, it slowly pivoted and silently floated from the harbor of their vision. At the terminal, another lively chain of hands and voices rejoined them to their baggage, settled them in a taxi, and carried them to the hotel. As Richard dropped six hundred-lira pieces into the driver's hand, they seemed the smoothest, roundest, most tactfully weighted coins he had ever given away. The hotel desk was one flight up. The clerk was young and playful. He pronounced their name several times, and wondered why they had not gone to Naples. The halls of the hotel, which had been described to them at the airport as second-class, were nevertheless of rose marble. The marble floor carried into their room. This, and the amplitude of the bathroom, and the imperial purple of the curtains blinded Richard to a serious imperfection until the clerk, his heels clicking in satisfaction with the perhaps miscalculated tip he had received, was far down the hall.

"Twin beds," Richard said. They had always had a double bed.

Joan asked, "Do you want to call him back?"

"How important is it to you?"

"I don't think it matters. Can you sleep alone?"

"I guess. But—" It was delicate. He felt they had been insulted. Until they finally parted, it seemed impertinent for anything, even a slice of space, to come between them. If this trip were to be kill or cure (and this was, for the tenth time, their slogan), then the attempt at a cure should have a certain technical purity, even though—or, rather, all the more because—in his heart he had already doomed it to fail. And also there was the material question of whether he could sleep without a warm proximate body to give his sleep shape.

"But what?" Joan prompted.

"But it seems sort of sad."

"Richard, don't be sad. You've been sad enough. You're supposed to relax. This isn't a honeymoon or anything, it's just a little rest we're trying to give each other. You can come visit me in my bed if you can't sleep."

"You're such a nice woman," he said. "I can't understand why I'm so miserable with you."

He had said this, or something like it, so often before that she, sickened by simultaneous doses of honey and gall, ignored the entire remark, and unpacked with a deliberate serenity. At her suggestion, they walked into the city, though it was ten o'clock. Their hotel was on a shopping street that at this hour was lined with lowered steel shutters. At the far end, an illuminated fountain played. His feet, which had never given him trouble, began to hurt. In the soft, damp air of the Roman winter, his shoes seemed to have developed hot inward convexities that gnashed his flesh at every stride. He could not imagine why this should be, unless he was allergic to marble. For the sake of his feet, they found an American bar, entered, and ordered coffee. Off in a corner, a drunken male American voice droned through the grooves of an unintelligible but distinctly female circuit of complaints; the voice, indeed, seemed not so much a man's as a woman's deepened by being played at a slower speed on the phonograph. Hoping to cure the growing dizzy emptiness within him, Richard ordered a "hamburger" that proved to be more tomato sauce than meat. Outside, on the street, he bought a paper cone of hot chestnuts from a sidewalk vendor. This man, whose thumbs and fingertips were charred black, agitated his hand until three hundred lire were placed in it. In a way, Richard welcomed being cheated; it gave him a place in the Roman economy. The Maples returned to the hotel, and side by side on their twin beds fell easily into a solid sleep.

That is, Richard assumed, in the cavernous accounting rooms of his subconscious, that Joan also slept well. But when they awoke in the morning, she told him, "You were terribly funny last night. I couldn't go to sleep, and every time I reached over to give you a little pat, to make you think you were in a double bed, you'd say 'Go away' and shake me off."

He laughed in delight. "Did I really? In my sleep?"

"It must have been. Once you shouted 'Leave me alone!' so loud I thought you must be awake, but when I tried to talk to you, you were snoring."

"Isn't that funny? I hope I didn't hurt your feelings."

"No. It was refreshing not to have you contradict yourself."

He brushed his teeth and ate a few of the cold chestnuts left over from the night before. The Maples breakfasted on hard rolls and bitter coffee in the hotel and walked again into Rome. His shoes resumed their inexplicable torture. With its strange, almost mocking attentiveness to their unseen needs, the city thrust a shoe store under their eyes; they entered, and Richard bought, from a gracefully reptilian young salesman, a pair of black alligator loafers. They were too tight, being smartly shaped, but they were dead—they did not pinch with the vital, outraged vehemence of the others. Then the Maples, she carrying the Hachette guidebook and he his American shoes in a box, walked down the

Via Nazionale to the Victor Emmanuel Monument, a titanic flight of stairs leading nowhere. "What was so great about him?" Richard asked. "Did he unify Italy? Or was that Cavour?"

"Is he the funny little king in *A Farewell to Arms?*"

"I don't know. But nobody could be *that* great."

"You can see now why the Italians don't have an inferiority complex. Everything is so huge."

They stood looking at the Palazzo Venezia until they imagined Mussolini frowning from a window, climbed the many steps to the Piazza del Campidoglio, and came to the equestrian statue of Marcus Aurelius on the pedestal by Michelangelo. Joan remarked how like a Marino Marini it was, and it was; her intuition had leaped eighteen centuries. She was so intelligent. Perhaps this was what made leaving her, as a gesture, so exquisite in conception and so difficult in execution. They circled the square. The portals and doors all around them seemed closed forever, like the doors in a drawing. They entered, because it was open, the side door of the church of Santa Maria in Aracoeli. They discovered themselves to be walking on sleeping people, life-size tomb-reliefs worn nearly featureless by footsteps. The fingers of the hands folded on the stone breasts had been smoothed to finger-shaped shadows. One face, sheltered from wear behind a pillar, seemed a vivid soul trying to rise from the all but erased body. Only the Maples examined these reliefs, cut into a floor that once must have been a glittering lake of mosaic; the other tourists clustered around the chapel preserving, in slippers and vestments, behind glass, the child-sized greenish remains of a pope. They left by the same side door and descended steps and paid admission to the ruins of the Roman Forum. The Renaissance had used it as a quarry; broken columns lay everywhere, loaded with perspective, like a de Chirico. Joan was charmed by the way birds and weeds lived in the crevices of this exploded civic dream. A delicate rain began to fall. At the end of one path, they peeked in glass doors, and a small uniformed man with a broom limped forward and admitted them, as if to a speakeasy, to the abandoned church of Santa Maria Antiqua. The pale vaulted air felt innocent of worship; the seventh-century frescoes seemed recently, nervously executed. As they left, Richard read the question in the broom man's smile and pressed a tactful coin into his hand. The gentle rain continued. Joan took Richard's arm, as if for shelter. His stomach began to hurt—a light, chafing ache at first, scarcely enough to distract him from the pain in his feet. They walked along the Via Sacra, through roofless pagan temples carpeted in grass. The ache in his stomach intensified. Uniformed guards, old men standing this way and that in the rain like hungry gulls, beckoned them toward further ruins, further churches, but the pain now had blinded Richard to everything but the extremity of his distance from anything that might give him support. He refused admittance to the Basilica of Constantine, and asked instead for the *uscita.* He did not feel capable of retracing his steps. The guard, seeing a source of tips escaping, dourly pointed toward a small gate in a nearby wire fence. The Maples lifted the latch, stepped through, and stood on the paved rise overlooking the Colosseum. Richard walked a little distance and leaned on a low wall.

"Is it so bad?" Joan asked.

"Oddly bad," he said. "I'm sorry. It's funny."

"Do you want to throw up?"

"No. It's not like that." His sentences came jerkily. "It's just a . . . sort of gripe."

"High or low?"

"In the middle."

"What could have caused it? The chestnuts?"

"No. It's just, I think, being here, so far from anywhere, with you, and not knowing . . . why."

"Shall we go back to the hotel?"

"Yes. I think if I could lie down."

"Shall we get a taxi?"

"They'll cheat me."

"That doesn't matter."

"I don't know . . . our address."

"We know sort of. It's near that big fountain. I'll look up the Italian for 'fountain.' "

"Rome is . . . full of . . . fountains."

"Richard. You aren't doing this just for my benefit?"

He had to laugh, she was so intelligent. "Not consciously. It has something to do . . . with having to hand out tips . . . all the time. It's really an ache. It's incredible."

"Can you walk?"

"Sure. Hold my arm."

"Shall I carry your shoebox?"

"No. Don't worry, sweetie. It's just a nervous ache. I used to get them . . . when I was little. But I was . . . braver then."

They descended steps to a thoroughfare thick with speeding traffic. The taxis they hailed carried heads in the rear and did not stop. They crossed the Via dei Fori Imperiali and tried to work their way back, against the sideways tug of interweaving streets, to the territory containing the fountain, the American bar, the shoe store, and the hotel. They passed through a market of bright food. Garlands of sausages hung from striped canopies. Heaps of lettuce lay in the street. He walked stiffly, as if the pain he carried were precious and fragile; holding one arm across his abdomen seemed to ease it slightly. The rain and Joan, having been in some way the pressures that had caused it, now became the pressures that enabled him to bear it. Joan kept him walking. The rain masked him, made his figure less distinct to passersby, and therefore less distinct to himself, and so dimmed his pain. The blocks seemed cruelly uphill and downhill. They climbed a long slope of narrow pavement beside the Banca d'Italia. The rain lifted. The pain, having expanded into every corner of the chamber beneath his ribs, had armed itself with a knife and now began to slash the walls in hope of escape. They reached the Via Nazionale, blocks below the hotel. The shops were unshuttered, the distant fountain was dry. He felt as if he were leaning backward, and his mind seemed a kind of twig, a twig that had deviated from the trunk and chosen to be this branch instead of that one, and chosen again and again, becoming finer with each choice, until finally there was nothing left for it but to vanish into air. In the hotel room he lay down on his twin bed, settled his overcoat over him, curled up, and fell asleep.

When he awoke an hour later, everything was different. The pain was gone. Joan was lying in her bed reading the Hachette guide. He saw her, as he rolled over, as if freshly, in the kind of cool library light in which he had first seen her; only he knew, calmly, that since then she had come to share his room. "It's gone," he told her.

"You're kidding. I was all set to call up a doctor and have you taken to a hospital."

"No, it wasn't anything like that. I knew it wasn't. It was nervous."

"You were dead white."

"It was too many different things focusing on the same spot. I think the Forum must have depressed me. The past here is so heavy. Also my shoes hurting bothered me."

"Darley, it's Rome. You're supposed to be happy."

"I am now. Come on. You must be starving. Let's get some lunch."

"Really? You feel up to it?"

"Quite. It's gone." And, except for a comfortable reminiscent soreness that the first swallow of Milanese salami healed, it was. The Maples embarked again upon Rome, and, in this city of steps, of sliding, unfolding perspectives, of many-windowed surfaces of sepia and rose ocher, of buildings so vast one seemed to be outdoors in them, the couple parted. Not physically—they rarely left each other's sight. But they had at last been parted. Both knew it. They became with each other, as in the days of courtship, courteous, gay, and quiet. Their marriage let go like an overgrown vine whose half-hidden stem had been slashed in the dawn by an ancient gardener. They walked arm in arm through seemingly solid blocks of buildings that parted, under examination, into widely separated slices of style and time. At one point she turned to him and said, "Darley, I know what was wrong with us. I'm classic, and you're baroque." They shopped, and saw, and slept, and ate. Sitting across from her in the last of the restaurants that like oases of linen and wine had sustained these level elegiac days, Richard saw that Joan was happy. Her face, released from the tension of hope, had grown smooth; her gestures had taken on the flirting irony of the young; she had become ecstatically attentive to everything about her; and her voice, as she bent forward to whisper a remark about a woman and a handsome man at another table, was rapid, as if the very air of her breathing had turned thin and free. She was happy, and, jealous of her happiness, he again grew reluctant to leave her.

Marching Through Boston

The civil-rights movement had a salubrious effect on Joan Maple. A suburban mother of four, she would return late at night from a nonviolence class in Roxbury with rosy cheeks and shining eyes, eager to describe, while sipping Benedictine, her indoctrination. "This huge man in overalls—"

"A Negro?" her husband asked.

"Of course, this huge man, with a *very* refined vocabulary, told us if we march anywhere, especially in the South, to let the Negro men march on the outside, because it's important for their self-esteem to be able to protect us. He told us about a

New York fashion designer who went down to Selma and said she could take care of herself. Furthermore she flirted with the state troopers. They finally asked her to come home."

"I thought you were supposed to love the troopers," Richard said.

"Only abstractly. Not on your own. You mustn't do *any*thing within the movement as an individual. By flirting, she gave the trooper an opportunity to feel contempt."

"She blocked his transference, as it were."

"Don't laugh. It's all very psychological. The man told us, those who want to go, to face our ego-gratificational motives no matter how irrelevant they are and then put them behind us. Once you're in a march, you have no identity. It's elegant. It's beautiful."

He had never known her like this. It seemed to Richard that her posture was improving, her figure filling out, her skin growing lustrous, her very hair gaining body and sheen. Though he had resigned himself, through twelve years of marriage, to a rhythm of apathy and renewal, he distrusted this raw burst of beauty.

The night she returned from Alabama, it was three o'clock in the morning. He woke and heard the front door close behind her. He had been dreaming of a parallelogram in the sky that was also somehow a meteor, and the darkened house seemed quadrisected by the four sleeping children he had, with more than paternal tenderness, put to bed. He had caught himself speaking to them of Mommy as a distant departed spirit, gone to live, invisible, in the newspapers and the television set. The little girl, Bean, had burst into tears. Now the ghost closed the door and walked up the stairs, and came into his bedroom, and fell on the bed.

He switched on the light and saw her sunburned face, her blistered feet. Her ballet slippers were caked with orange mud. She had lived for three days on Coke and dried apricots; she had not gone to the bathroom for sixteen hours. The Montgomery airport had been a madhouse—nuns, social workers, divinity students fighting for space on the northbound planes. They had been in the air when they heard about Mrs. Liuzzo.

He accused her: "It could have been you."

She said, "I was always in a group." But she added guiltily, "How were the children?"

"Fine. Bean cried because she thought you were inside the television set."

"Did you see me?"

"Your parents called long distance to say they thought they did. I didn't. All I saw was Abernathy and King and their henchmen saying, 'Thass right. Say it, man. Thass sayin' it.' "

"Aren't you mean? It was very moving, except that we were all so tired. These teen-age Negro girls kept fainting; a psychiatrist explained to me that they were having psychotic breaks."

"What psychiatrist?"

"Actually, there were three of them, and they were studying to be psychiatrists in Philadelphia. They kind of took me in tow."

"I bet they did. Please come to bed. I'm very tired from being a mother."

She visited the four corners of the upstairs to inspect each sleeping child and, returning, undressed in the dark. She removed underwear she had worn for seventy hours and stood there shining; to the sleepy man in the bed it seemed a visitation, and he felt as people of old must have felt when greeted by an angel—adoring yet resentful, at this flamboyant proof of better things.

She spoke on the radio; she addressed local groups. In garages and supermarkets he heard himself being pointed out as her husband. She helped organize meetings at which dapper young Negroes ridiculed and abused the applauding suburban audience. Richard marveled at Joan's public composure. Her shyness stayed with her, but it had become a kind of weapon, as if the doctrine of nonviolence had given it point. Her voice, as she phoned evasive local realtors in the campaign for fair housing, grew curiously firm and rather obstinately melodious—a note her husband had never heard in her voice before. He grew jealous and irritable. He found himself insisting, at parties, on the Constitutional case for states' rights, on the misfortunes of African independence, on the tangled history of the Reconstruction. Yet she had little trouble persuading him to march with her in Boston.

He promised, though he could not quite grasp the object of the march. Indeed, his brain, as if surgically deprived, quite lacked the faculty of believing in people considered generically. All movements, of masses or of ideas supposedly embodied in masses, he secretly felt to be phantasmal. Whereas his wife, a minister's daughter, lived by abstractions; her blood returned to her heart enriched and vivified by the passage through some capillarious figment. He was struck, and subtly wounded, by the ardor with which she rewarded his promise; under his hands her body felt baroque and her skin smooth as night.

The march was in April. Richard awoke that morning with a fever. He had taken something foreign into himself and his body was making resistance. Joan offered to go alone; as if something fundamental to his dignity, to their marriage, were at stake, he refused the offer. The day, dawning cloudy, had been forecast as sunny, and he wore a summer suit that enclosed his hot skin in a slipping, weightless unreality. At a highway drugstore they bought some pills designed to detonate inside him through a twelve-hour period. They parked near her aunt's house in Louisburg Square and took a taxi toward the headwaters of the march, a playground in Roxbury. The Irish driver's impassive back radiated disapproval. The cab was turned aside by a policeman; the Maples got out and walked down a broad brown boulevard lined with barbershops, shoe-repair nooks, pizzerias, and friendliness associations. On stoops and stairways male Negroes loitered, blinking and muttering toward one another as if a vast, decrepit conspiracy had assigned them their positions and then collapsed.

"Lovely architecture," Joan said, pointing toward a curving side street, a neo-Georgian arc suspended in the large urban sadness.

Though she pretended to know where she was, Richard doubted that they were going the right way. But then he saw ahead of them, scattered like the anomalous objects with which Dali punctuates his perspectives, receding black groups of white clergymen. In the distance, the hot lights of police cars wheeled within a twinkling mob. As they drew nearer, colored girls made into giantesses by bouffant hairdos materialized beside them. One wore cerise stretch pants and the golden sandals of a heavenly cupbearer, and held pressed against her ear a transistor radio tuned to WMEX. On this thin stream of music they all together poured into a playground surrounded by a link fence.

A loose crowd of thousands swarmed on the crushed grass. Bobbing placards advertised churches, brotherhoods, schools, towns. Popsicle vendors lent an unexpected touch of carnival. Suddenly at home, Richard bought a bag of peanuts and looked around—as if this were the playground of his childhood—for friends.

But it was Joan who found some. "My God," she said. "There's my old analyst." At the fringe of some Unitarians stood a plump, doughy man with the troubled squint of a baker who has looked into too many ovens. Joan turned to go the other way.

"Don't suppress," Richard told her. "Let's go and be friendly and normal."

"It's too embarrassing."

"But it's been years since you went. You're cured."

"You don't understand. You're never cured. You just stop going."

"O.K., come this way. I think I see my Harvard section man in Plato to Dante."

But, even while arguing against it, she had been

drifting them toward her psychiatrist, and now they were caught in the pull of his gaze. He scowled and came toward them, flat-footedly. Richard had never met him and, shaking hands, felt himself as a putrid heap of anecdotes, of detailed lusts and abuses. "I think I need a doctor," he madly blurted.

The other man produced, like a stiletto from his sleeve, a nimble smile. "How so?" Each word seemed precious.

"I have a fever."

"Ah." The psychiatrist turned sympathetically to Joan, and his face issued a clear commiseration: *So he is still punishing you.*

Joan said loyally, "He really does. I saw the thermometer."

"Would you like a peanut?" Richard asked. The offer felt so symbolic, so transparent, that he was shocked when the other man took one, cracked it harshly, and substantially chewed.

Joan asked, "Are you with anybody? I feel a need for group security."

"Come meet my sister." The command sounded strange to Richard; "sister" seemed a piece of psychological slang, a euphemism for "mistress."

But again things were simpler than they seemed. His sister was plainly from the same batter. Ruddy and yeasty, she seemed to have been enlarged by the exercise of good will and wore a saucer-sized S.C.L.C. button in the lapel of a coarse green suit. Richard coveted the suit; it looked warm. The day was continuing overcast and chilly. Something odd, perhaps the successive explosions of the antihistamine pill, was happening inside him, making him feel elegantly elongated; the illusion crossed his mind that he was destined to seduce this woman. She beamed and said, "My daughter Trudy and her *best* friend, Carol."

They were girls of sixteen or so, one size smaller in their bones than women. Trudy had the family pastry texture and a darting frown. Carol was homely, fragile, and touching; her upper teeth were a gray blur of braces and her arms were protectively folded across her skimpy bosom. Over a white blouse she wore only a thin blue sweater, unbuttoned. Richard told her, "You're freezing."

"I'm freezing," she said, and a small love was established between them on the basis of this demure repetition. She added, "I came along because I'm writing a term paper."

Trudy said, "She's doing a history of the labor unions," and laughed unpleasantly.

The girl shivered. "I thought they might be the same. Didn't the unions use to march?" Her voice, moistened by the obtrusion of her braces, had a sprayey faintness in the raw gray air.

The psychiatrist's sister said, "The *way* they *make* these poor children *study* nowadays! The *books* they have them *read!* Their *English* teacher *assigned* them *Tropic of Cancer!* I picked it *up* and read *one page,* and Trudy reassured me, 'It's all *right,* Mother, the teacher says he's a Transcen-*dent*alist!' "

It felt to Richard less likely that he would seduce her. His sense of reality was expanding in the nest of warmth these people provided. He offered to buy them all Popsicles. His consciousness ventured outward and tasted the joy of so many Negro presences, the luxury of immersion in the polished shadows of their skins. He drifted happily through the crosshatch of their oblique sardonic hooting and blurred voices, searching for the Popsicle vendor. The girls and Trudy's mother had said they would take one; the psychiatrist and Joan had refused. The crowd was formed of jiggling fragments. Richard waved at the rector of a church whose nursery school his children had attended; winked at a folk singer he had seen on television and who looked lost and wan in depth; assumed a stony face in passing a long-haired youth guarded by police and draped in a signboard proclaiming MARTIN LUTHER KING A TOOL OF THE COMMUNISTS; and tapped a tall bald man on the shoulder. "Remember me? Dick Maple, Plato to Dante, B-plus."

The section man turned, bespectacled and pale. It was shocking; he had aged.

The march was slow to start. Trucks and police cars appeared and disappeared at the playground gate. Officious young seminarians tried to organize the crowd into lines. Unintelligible announcements crackled within the loudspeakers. Martin Luther King was a dim religious rumor on the playground plain—now here, now there, now dead, now alive. The sun showed as a kind of sore spot burning through the clouds. Carol nibbled her Popsicle and shivered. Richard and Joan argued whether to march under the Danvers banner with the psychiatrist or with the Unitarians because her father was one. In the end it did not matter; King invisibly established himself at their head, a distant truck loaded with singing women lurched forward, a far corner of the crowd began to croon, "Which side are you on, boy?," and they were marching.

On Columbus Avenue they were shuffled into lines ten abreast. The Maples were separated. Joan turned up between her psychiatrist and a massive, doleful African wearing tribal scars, sneakers, and a Harvard Athletic Association sweatshirt. Richard found himself at the end of the line ahead, with Carol beside him. The man behind him, a forward-looking liberal, stepped on his heel, giving the knit of his loafer such a wrench that he had to walk the three miles through Boston with a floppy shoe and a dragging limp. He had been born in West Virginia, near the Pennsylvania line, and did not understand Boston. In ten years he had grown familiar with some of its districts, but was still surprised by the quick curving manner in which these districts interlocked. For a few blocks they marched between cheering tenements from whose topmost windows hung banners that proclaimed END DE FACTO SEGREGATION and RETIRE MRS. HICKS. Then the march turned left, and Richard was passing Symphony Hall, within whose rectangular vault he had often dreamed his way along the deep-grassed meadows of Brahms and up the agate cliffs of Strauss. At this corner, from the Stygian subway kiosk, he had emerged with Joan, Orpheus and Eurydice, when both were students; in this restaurant, a decade later, he and she, on four drinks apiece, had decided not to get a divorce that week. The new Prudential Tower, taller and somehow fainter than any other building, haunted each twist of their march, before their faces like a mirage, at their backs like a memory. A leggy nervous colored girl wearing the orange fireman's jacket of the Security Unit shepherded their section of the line, clapping her hands, shouting freedom-song lyrics for a few bars. These songs struggled through the miles of the march, overlapping and eclipsing one another. "Which side are you on, boy, which side are you on . . . like a tree-ee planted by the wah-hater, we shall not be moved . . . this little light of mine, gonna shine on Boston, Mass., this little light of mine . . ." The day continued cool and without shadows. Newspapers that he had folded inside his coat for warmth slipped and slid. Carol beside him plucked at her little sweater, gathering it at her breast but unable, as if under a spell, to button it. Behind him, Joan, serenely framed between her id and superego, stepped along masterfully, swinging her arms, throwing her ballet slippers alternately outward in a confident splaying stride. ". . . let 'er shine, let 'er shine . . ."

Incredibly, they were traversing a cloverleaf, an elevated concrete arabesque devoid of cars. Their massed footsteps whispered; the city yawned beneath them. The march had no beginning and no end that Richard could see. Within him, the fever had become a small glassy scratching on the walls of the pit hollowed by the detonating pills. A piece of newspaper spilled down his legs and blew into the air. Impalpably medicated, ideally motivated, he felt, strolling along the curve of the cloverleaf, gathered within an irresistible ascent. He asked Carol, "Where are we going?"

"The newspapers said the Common."

"Do you feel faint?"

Her gray braces shyly modified her smile. "Hungry."

"Have a peanut." A few still remained in his pocket.

"Thank you." She took one. "You don't have to be paternal."

"I want to be." He felt strangely exalted and excited, as if destined to give birth. He wanted to share this sensation with Carol, but instead he asked her, "In your study of the labor movement, have you learned much about the Molly Maguires?"

"No. Were they goons or finks?"

"I think they were either coal miners or gangsters."

"Oh. I haven't studied about anything earlier than Gompers."

"I think you're wise." Suppressing the urge to tell her he loved her, he turned to look at Joan. She was beautiful, in the style of a poster, with far-seeing blue eyes and red lips parted in song.

Now they walked beneath office buildings where like mounted butterflies secretaries and dental technicians were pressed against the glass. In Copley Square, stony shoppers waited forever to cross the street. Along Boylston, there was Irish muttering; he shielded Carol with his body. The desultory singing grew defiant. The Public Garden was beginning to bloom. Worthy statues—Channing, Kosciusko, Cass, Phillips—were trundled by beneath the blurring trees; Richard's dry heart cracked like a book being opened. The march turned left down Charles and began to press against itself, to link arms, to fumble for love. He lost sight of Joan in the crush. Then they were treading on grass, on the Common, and the first drops of rain, sharp as needles, pricked their faces and hands.

"Did we have to stay to hear every damn speech?" Richard asked. They were at last heading home; he felt too sick to drive and huddled, in his soaked slippery suit, toward the heater. The windshield wiper seemed to be squeaking *free-dom, free-dom.*

"I wanted to hear King."

"You heard him in Alabama."

"I was too tired to listen then."

"Did you listen this time? Didn't it seem corny and forced?"

"Somewhat. But does it matter?" Her white profile was serene; she passed a trailer truck on the right, and her window was spattered as if with applause.

"And that Abernathy. God, if he's John the Baptist, I'm Herod the Great. 'Onteel de Frenchman go back t' France, onteel de Ahrishman go back t' Ahrland, onteel de Mexican he go back tuh—' "

"Stop it."

"Don't get me wrong. I didn't mind them sounding like demagogues; what I minded was that godawful boring phony imitation of a revival meeting. 'Thass right, yossuh. Yoh-*suh!*' "

"Your throat sounds sore. Shouldn't you stop using it?"

"*How* could you crucify me that way? *How* could you make this miserable sick husband stand in the icy rain for hours listening to boring stupid speeches that you'd heard before anyway?"

"I didn't think the speeches were that great. But I think it was important that they were given and that people listened. You were there as a witness, Richard."

"Ah witnessed. Ah believes. Yos-suh."

"You're a very sick man."

"I know, I *know* I am. That's why I wanted to leave. Even your pasty psychiatrist left. He looked like a dunked doughnut."

"He left because of the girls."

"I loved Carol. She respected me, despite the color of my skin."

"You didn't have to go."

"Yes I did. You somehow turned it into a point of honor. It was a sexual vindication."

"How you go on."

" 'Onteel de East German goes on back t' East Germany, onteel de Luxembourgian hies hisself back to Luxembourg—' "

"Please stop it."

But he found he could not stop, and even after they reached home and she put him to bed, the children watching in alarm, his voice continued its slurred plaint. "Ah'ze all riaight, Missy, jes' a tech o' double pneu*mon*ia, don't you fret none, we'll get the cotton in."

"You're embarrassing the children."

"Shecks, doan min' me, chilluns. Ef Ah could jes' res' hyah foh a spell in de shade o' de watuh-melon patch, res' dese ol' bones . . . Lawzy, dat do feel good!"

"Daddy has a tiny cold," Joan explained.

"Will he die?" Bean asked, and burst into tears.

"Now, effen," he said, "bah some un*foh*-choonut chayance, mah spirrut should pass owen, bureh me bah de levee, so mebbe Ah kin heeah de singin' an' de banjos an' de cotton bolls a-bustin' . . . an' mebbe even de whaat folks up in de Big House kin shed a homely tear er two . . ." He was almost crying; a weird tenderness had crept over him in bed, as if he had indeed given birth, birth to this voice, a voice crying for attention from the depths of oppression. High in the window, the late afternoon sky blanched as the storm lifted. In the warmth of the bed, Richard crooned to himself, and once started up, crying out, "Missy! Missy! Doan you worreh none, ol' Tom'll see anotheh sun-up!"

But Joan was downstairs, talking firmly on the telephone.

The Taste of Metal

Metal, strictly, has no taste; its presence in the mouth is felt as disciplinary, as a *No* spoken to other tastes. When Richard Maple, after thirty years of twinges, jagged edges, and occasional extractions, had all his remaining molars capped and bridges shaped across the gaps, the gold felt chilly to his cheeks and its regularity masked holes and roughnesses that had been a kind of mirror wherein his tongue had known itself. The Friday of the final cementing, he went to a small party. As he drank a variety of liquids that tasted much the same, he moved from feeling slightly less than himself (his native teeth had been ground to stumps of dentine) to feeling slightly more. The shift in tonality that permeated his skull whenever his jaws closed corresponded, perhaps, to the heightened clarity that fills the mind after a religious conversion. He saw his companions at the party with a new brilliance—a sharpness of vision that, like a camera's, was specific and restricted in focus. He could see only one person at a time, and found himself focusing less on his wife Joan than on Eleanor Dennis, the long-legged wife of a municipal-bond salesman.

Eleanor's distinctness in part had to do with the legal fact that she and her husband were "separated." It had happened recently; his absence from the party was noticeable. Eleanor, in the course of a life that she described as a series of harrowing survivals, had developed the brassy social manner that converts private catastrophe into public humorousness; but tonight her agitation was imperfectly converted. She listened as if for an echo that wasn't there, and twitchily crossed and recrossed her legs. Her legs were handsome and vivid and so long that, after midnight, when parlor games began, she hitched up her brief skirt and kicked the lintel of a doorframe. The host balanced a glass of water on his forehead. Richard, demonstrating a headstand, mistakenly tumbled forward, delighted at his own softness, which he felt to be an ironical comment upon flesh that his new metal teeth were making. He was all mortality, all porous erosion save for these stars in his head, an impervious polar cluster at the zenith of his slow whirling.

His wife came to him with a face as neat and unscarred as the face of a clock. It was time to go home. And Eleanor needed a ride. The three of them, plus the hostess in her bangle earrings and coffee-stained culottes, went to the door, and discovered a snowstorm. As far as the eye could probe, flakes were falling in a jostling crowd through the whispering lavender night. "God bless us, every one," Richard said.

The hostess suggested that Joan should drive.

Richard kissed her on the cheek and tasted the metal of her bitter earring and got in behind the wheel. His car was a brand-new Corvair; he wouldn't dream of trusting anyone else to drive it. Joan crawled into the back seat, grunting to emphasize the physical awkwardness, and Eleanor serenely arranged her coat and pocketbook and legs in the space beside him. The motor sprang alive. Richard felt resiliently cushioned: Eleanor was beside him, Joan behind him, God above him, the road beneath him. The fast-falling snow dipped brilliant—explosive, chrysanthemumesque—into the car headlights. On a small hill the tires spun—a loose, reassuring noise, like the slither of a raincoat.

In the knobbed darkness lit by the green speed gauge, Eleanor, showing a wealth of knee, talked at length of her separated husband. "You have no *idea,*" she said, "you two are so sheltered you have no idea what men are capable of. I didn't know myself. I don't mean to sound ungracious, he gave me nine reasonable years and I wouldn't *dream* of punishing him with the children's visiting hours the way some women would, but that *man!* You know what he had the crust to tell me? He actually told me that when he was with another woman he'd sometimes close his eyes and pretend it was *me.*"

"Sometimes," Richard said.

His wife behind him said, "Darley, are you aware that the road is slippery?"

"That's the shine of the headlights," he told her.

Eleanor crossed and recrossed her legs. Half the length of a thigh flared in the intimate green glow. She went on, "And his *trips.* I wondered why the same city was always putting out bond issues. I began to feel sorry for the mayor, I thought they were going bankrupt. Looking back at myself, I was so *good,* so wrapped up in the children and the house, always on the phone to the contractor or the plumber or the gas company trying to get the new kitchen done in time for Thanksgiving when his silly, *silly* mother was coming to visit. About once a day I'd sharpen the carving knife. Thank God that phase of my life is over. I went to his mother for sympathy I suppose and very indignantly she asked me, What had I done to her boy? The children and I had tuna-fish sandwiches by ourselves and it was the first Thanksgiving I've ever enjoyed, frankly."

"I always have trouble," Richard told her, "finding the second joint."

Joan said, "Darley, you know you're coming to that terrible curve?"

"You should see my father-in-law carve. Snick, snap, snap, snick. Your blood runs cold."

"On my birthday, my *birth*day," Eleanor said, accidentally kicking the heater, "the bastard was with his little dolly in a restaurant, and he told me, he solemnly told me—men are incredible—he told me he ordered cake for dessert. That was his tribute to me. The night he confessed all this, it was the end of the world, but I had to laugh. I asked him if he'd had the restaurant put a candle on the cake. He told me he'd thought of it but hadn't had the guts."

Richard's responsive laugh was held in suspense as the car skidded on the curve. A dark upright shape had appeared in the center of the windshield, and he tried to remove it, but the automobile proved impervious to the steering wheel and instead drew closer, as if magnetized, to a telephone pole that rigidly insisted on its position in the center of the windshield. The pole enlarged. The little splinters pricked by the linemen's cleats leaped forward in the headlights, and there was a flat whack surprisingly unambiguous, considering how casually it had happened. Richard felt the sudden refusal of motion, the *No,* and knew, though his mind was deeply cushioned in a cottony indifference, that an event had occurred which in another incarnation he would regret.

"You jerk," Joan said. Her voice was against his ear. "Your pretty new car." She asked, "Eleanor, are you all right?" With a rising inflection she repeated, "Are you all right?" It sounded like scolding.

Eleanor giggled softly, embarrassed. "I'm fine," she said, "except that I can't seem to move my legs." The windshield near her head had become a web of light, an exploded star.

Either the radio had been on or had turned itself on, for mellow, meditating music flowed from a realm behind time. Richard identified it as one of Handel's oboe sonatas. He noticed that his knees distantly hurt. Eleanor had slid forward and seemed unable to uncross her legs. Shockingly, she whimpered. Joan asked, "Sweetheart, didn't you know you were going too fast?"

"I am very stupid," he said. Music and snow poured down upon them, and he imagined that, if only the oboe sonata were played backwards, they would leap backwards from the telephone pole and be on their way home again. The little distances to their houses, once measured in minutes, had frozen and become immense.

Using her hands, Eleanor uncrossed her legs and brought herself upright in her seat. She lit a cigarette. Richard, his knees creaking, got out of the car and tried to push it free. He told Joan to come out of the back seat and get behind the wheel. Their motions were clumsy, wriggling in and out of darkness. The headlights still burned, but the beams were bent inward, toward each other. The Corvair had a hollow head, its engine being in the rear. Its face, an unimpassioned insect's face, was inextricably curved around the pole; the bumper had become locked mandibles. When Richard pushed and Joan fed gas, the wheels whined in a vacuum. The smooth encircling night extended around them, above and beyond the snow. No window light had acknowledged their accident.

Joan, who had a social conscience, asked, "Why doesn't anybody come out and help us?"

Eleanor, the voice of bitter experience, answered,

"This pole is hit so often it's just a nuisance to the neighborhood."

Richard announced, "I'm too drunk to face the police." The remark hung with a neon clarity in the night.

A car came by, slowed, stopped. A window rolled down and revealed a frightened male voice. "Everything O.K.?"

"Not entirely," Richard said. He was pleased by his powers, under stress, of exact expression.

"I can take somebody to a telephone. I'm on my way back from a poker game."

A lie, Richard reasoned—otherwise, why advance it? The boy's face had the blurred pallor of the sexually drained. Taking care to give each word weight, Richard told him, "One of us can't move and I better stay with her. If you could take my wife to a phone, we'd all be most grateful."

"Who do I call?" Joan asked.

Richard hesitated between the party they had left, their babysitter at home, and Eleanor's husband, who was living in a motel on Route 128.

The boy answered for him: "The police."

As Iphigenia redeemed the becalmed fleet at Aulis, so Joan got into the stranger's car, a rusty red Mercury. The car faded through the snow, which was slackening. The storm had been just a flurry, an illusion conjured to administer this one rebuke. It wouldn't even make tomorrow's newspapers.

Richard's knees felt as if icicles were being pressed against the soft spot beneath the caps, where the doctor's hammer searches for a reflex. He got in behind the wheel again, and switched off the lights. He switched off the ignition. Eleanor's cigarette glowed. Though his system was still adrift in liquor, he could not quite forget the taste of metal in his teeth. That utterly flat *No:* through several dreamlike thicknesses something very hard had touched him. Once, swimming in surf, he had been sucked under by a large wave. Tons of sudden surge had enclosed him and, with an implacable downward shrug, thrust him deep into dense green bitterness and stripped him of weight; his struggling became nothing, he was nothing within the wave. There had been no hatred. The wave simply hadn't *cared.*

He tried to apologize to the woman beside him in the darkness.

She said, "Oh, please. I'm sure nothing's broken. At the worst I'll be on crutches for a few days." She laughed and added, "This just isn't my year."

"Does it hurt?"

"No, not at all."

"You're probably in shock. You'll be cold. I'll

get the heat back." Richard was sobering, and an infinite drabness was dawning for him. Never again, never ever, would his car be new, would he chew on his own enamel, would she kick so high with her vivid long legs. He turned the ignition back on and started up the motor, for warmth. The radio softly returned, still Handel.

Moving from the hips up with surprising strength, Eleanor turned and embraced him. Her cheeks were wet; her lipstick tasted manufactured. Searching for her waist, for the smallness of her breasts, he fumbled through thicknesses of cloth. They were still in each other's arms when the whirling blue light of the police car broke upon them.

Your Lover Just Called

The telephone rang, and Richard Maple, who had stayed home from work this Friday because of a cold, answered it: "Hello?" The person at the other end of the line hung up. Richard went into the bedroom, where Joan was making the bed, and said, "Your lover just called."

"What did he say?"

"Nothing. He hung up. He was amazed to find me home."

"Maybe it was *your* lover."

He knew, through the phlegm beclouding his head, that there was something wrong with this, and found it. "If it was *my* lover," he said, "why would she hang up, since I answered?"

Joan shook the sheet so it made a clapping noise. "Maybe she doesn't love you anymore."

"This is a ridiculous conversation."

"You started it."

"Well, what would *you* think, if you answered the phone on a weekday and the person hung up? He clearly expected you to be home alone."

"Well, if you'll go to the store for cigarettes I'll call him back and explain what happened."

"You think I'll think you're kidding but I know that's really what *would* happen."

"Oh, come on, Dick. Who would it be? Freddie Vetter?"

"Or Harry Saxon. Or somebody I don't know at all. Some old college friend who's moved to New England. Or maybe the milkman. I can hear you and him talking while I'm shaving sometimes."

"We're surrounded by hungry children. He's fifty years old and has hair coming out of his ears."

"Like your father. You're not adverse to older men. There was that Chaucer section man when we first met. Anyway, you've been acting awfully happy lately. There's a little smile comes into your face when you're doing the housework. See, there it is!"

"I'm smiling," Joan said, "because you're so absurd. I have no lover. I have nowhere to put him. My days are consumed by devotion to the needs of my husband and his many children."

"Oh, so I'm the one who made you have all the children? While you were hankering after a career in fashion or in the exciting world of business. Aeronautics, perhaps. You could have been the first woman to design a titanium nose cone. Or to crack the wheat-futures cycle. Joan Maple, girl agronomist. Joan Maple, lady geopolitician. But for that fornicating brute she mistakenly married, this clear-eyed female citizen of our ever-needful republic—"

"Dick, have you taken your temperature? I haven't heard you rave like this for years."

"I haven't been betrayed like this for years. I hated that *click.* That nasty little I-know-your-wife-better-than-you-do *click.*"

"It was some child. If we're going to have Mack for dinner tonight, you better convalesce now."

"It *is* Mack, isn't it? That son of a bitch. The divorce isn't even finalized and he's calling my wife on the phone. And then proposes to gorge himself at my groaning board."

"I'll be groaning myself. You're giving me a headache."

"Sure. First I foist off children on you in my mad desire for progeny, then I give you a menstrual headache."

"Get into bed and I'll bring you orange juice and toast cut into strips the way your mother used to make it."

"You're lovely."

As he was settling himself under the blankets, the phone rang again, and Joan answered it in the upstairs hall. "Yes . . . no . . . no . . . good," she said, and hung up.

"Who was it?" he called.

"Somebody wanting to sell us the *World Book Encyclopedia,*" she called back.

"A very likely story," he said, with self-pleasing irony, leaning back onto the pillows confident that he was being unjust, that there was no lover.

Mack Dennis was a homely, agreeable, sheepish man their age, whose wife, Eleanor, was in Wyoming suing for divorce. He spoke of her with a cloying tenderness, as if of a favorite daughter away for the first time at camp, or as a departed angel nevertheless keeping in close electronic touch with the scorned earth. "She says they've had some wonderful thunderstorms. The children go horseback riding every morning, and they play Pounce at night and are in bed by ten. Everybody's health has never been better. Ellie's asthma has cleared up and she thinks now she must have been allergic to *me.*"

"You should have cut all your hair off and dressed in cellophane," Richard told him.

Joan asked him, "And how's *your* health? Are you feeding yourself enough? Mack, you look thin."

"The nights I don't stay in Boston," Mack said, tapping himself all over for a pack of cigarettes, "I've taken to eating at the motel on Route 33. It's the best food in town now, and you can watch the kids in the swimming pool." He studied his empty upturned hands as if they had recently held a surprise. He missed his own kids, was perhaps the surprise.

"I'm out of cigarettes too," Joan said.

"I'll go get some," Richard said.

"And a thing of Bitter Lemon at the liquor store."

"I'll make a pitcher of Martinis," Mack said. "Doesn't it feel great, to have Martini weather again?"

It was that season which is late summer in the days and early autumn at night. Evening descended on the downtown, lifting the neon tubing into brilliance, as Richard ran his errand. His sore throat felt folded within him like a secret; there was something reckless and gay in his being up and out at all after spending the afternoon in bed. Home, he parked by his back fence and walked down through a lawn loud with fallen leaves, though the trees overhead were still massy. The lit windows of his house looked golden and idyllic; the children's rooms were above (the face of Judith, his bigger daughter, drifted preoccupied across a slice of her wallpaper, and her pink square hand reached to adjust a doll on a shelf) and the kitchen below. In the kitchen windows, whose tone was fluorescent, a silent tableau was being enacted. Mack was holding a Martini shaker and pouring it into a vessel, eclipsed by an element of window sash, that Joan was offering with a long white arm. Head tilted winningly, she was talking with the slightly pushed-forward mouth that Richard recognized as peculiar to her while looking into mirrors, conversing with her elders, or otherwise trying to display herself to advantage. Whatever she was saying made Mack laugh, so that his pouring (the silver shaker head glinted, a drop of greenish liquid spilled) was unsteady. He set the shaker down and displayed his hands—the same hands from which a little while ago a surprise had seemed to escape—at his sides, shoulder-high. Joan moved toward him, still holding her glass, and the back of her head, done up taut and oval in a bun, with blond down trailing at the nape of her neck, eclipsed all of Mack's face but his eyes, which closed. They were kissing. Joan's head tilted one way and Mack's another to make their mouths meet tighter. The graceful line of her shoulders was carried outward by the line of the arm holding her glass safe in the air. The other arm was around his neck. Behind them an open cabinet door revealed a paralyzed row of erect paper boxes whose lettering Richard could not read but whose coloring advertised their contents—Cheerios, Wheat Honeys, Onion Thins. Joan backed off and ran her index finger down the length of Mack's necktie (a summer tartan), ending with a jab in the vicinity of his navel that might have expressed a rebuke or a regret. His face, pale and lumpy in the harsh vertical light, looked mildly humorous but intent, and moved forward, toward hers, an inch or two. The scene had the fascinating slow motion of action underwater, mixed with the insane silent suddenness of a television montage glimpsed from the street. Judith came to the window upstairs, not noticing her father standing in the massy shadow of the tree. Wearing a nightie of lemon gauze, she innocently scratched her armpit while studying a moth beating on her screen; and this too gave Richard a momentous sense, crowding his heart, of having been brought by the mute act of witnessing—like a child sitting alone at the movies—perilously close to the hidden machinations of things. In another kitchen window a neglected teakettle began to plume and to fog the panes with steam. Joan was talking again; her forward-thrust lips seemed to be throwing rapid little bridges across a narrowing gap. Mack paused, shrugged; his face puckered as if he were speaking French. Joan's head snapped back with laughter and triumphantly she threw her free arm wide and was in his embrace again. His hand, spread starlike on the small of her back, went lower to what, out of sight behind the edge of Formica counter, would be her bottom.

Richard scuffled loudly down the cement steps and kicked the kitchen door open, giving them time to break apart before he entered. From the far end of the kitchen, smaller than children, they looked at him with blurred, blank expressions. Joan turned off the steaming kettle and Mack shambled forward to pay for the cigarettes. After the third round of Martinis, the constraints loosened and Richard said, taking pleasure in the plaintive huskiness of his voice, "Imagine my discomfort. Sick as I am, I go out into this bitter night to get my wife and my guest some cigarettes, so they can pollute the air and aggravate my already grievous bronchial condition, and coming down through the back yard, what do I see? The two of them doing the Kama Sutra in my own kitchen. It was like seeing a blue movie and knowing the people in it."

"Where do you see blue movies nowadays?" Joan asked.

"Tush, Dick," Mack said sheepishly, rubbing his thighs with a brisk ironing motion. "A mere fraternal kiss. A brotherly hug. A disinterested tribute to your wife's charm."

"Really, Dick," Joan said. "I think it's shockingly sneaky of you to be standing around spying into your own windows."

"Standing around! I was transfixed with horror. It was a real trauma. My first primal scene." A profound happiness was stretching him from within; the reach of his tongue and wit felt immense, and the other two seemed dolls, homunculi, in his playful grasp.

"We were hardly doing anything," Joan said, lifting her head as if to rise above it all, the lovely line of her jaw defined by tension, her lips stung by a pout.

"Oh, I'm sure, by your standards, you had hardly begun. You'd hardly sampled the possible wealth of coital positions. Did you think I'd never return? Have you poisoned my drink and I'm too vigorous to die, like Rasputin?"

"Dick," Mack said, "Joan loves you. And if I love any man, it's you. Joan and I had this out years ago, and decided to be merely friends."

"Don't go Irish on me, Mack Dennis. 'If I love any mon, 'tis thee.' Don't give me a thought, laddie. Just think of poor Eleanor out there, sweating out your divorce, bouncing up and down on those horses day after day, playing Pounce till she's black and blue—"

"Let's eat," Joan said. "You've made me so nervous I've probably overdone the roast beef. Really, Dick, I don't think you can excuse yourself by trying to make it funny."

Next day, the Maples awoke soured and dazed by hangovers; Mack had stayed until two, to make sure there were no hard feelings. Joan usually played ladies' tennis Saturday mornings, while Richard amused the children; now, dressed in white shorts and sneakers, she delayed at home in order to quarrel. "It's desperate of you," she told Richard, "to try to make something of Mack and me. What are you trying to cover up?"

"My dear Mrs. Maple, I *saw*," he said. "I *saw* through my own windows you doing a very credible impersonation of a female spider having her abdomen tickled. Where did you learn to flirt your head like that? It was better than finger puppets."

"Mack always kisses me in the kitchen. It's a habit, it means nothing. You know for yourself how in love with Eleanor he is."

"So much he's divorcing her. His devotion verges on the quixotic."

"The divorce is her idea, you know that. He's a lost soul. I feel sorry for him."

"Yes, I saw that you do. You were like the Red Cross at Verdun."

"What I'd like to know is, why are you so pleased?"

"Pleased? I'm annihilated."

"You're delighted. Look at your smile in the mirror."

"You're so incredibly unapologetic, I guess I think you must be being ironical."

The telephone rang. Joan picked it up and said, "Hello," and Richard heard the click across the room. Joan replaced the receiver and said to him, "So. She thought I'd be playing tennis by now."

"Who's she?"

"You tell me. Your lover. Your loveress."

"It was clearly yours, and something in your voice warned him off."

"Go to her!" Joan suddenly cried, with a burst of the same defiant energy that made her, on other hungover mornings, rush through a mountain of housework. "Go to her like a man and stop trying to maneuver me into something I don't understand! I have no lover! I let Mack kiss me because he's lonely and drunk! Stop trying to make me more interesting than I am! All I am is a beat-up housewife who wants to go play tennis with some other tired ladies!"

Mutely Richard fetched from their sports closet

her tennis racket, which had recently been restrung with gut. Carrying it in his mouth like a dog retrieving a stick, he laid it at the toe of her sneaker. Richard Jr., their older son, a wiry nine-year-old presently obsessed by the accumulation of Batman cards, came into the living room, witnessed this pantomime, and laughed to hide his fright. "Dad, can I have my nickel for emptying the wastebaskets?"

"Mommy's going to go out to play, Dickie," Richard said, licking from his lips the salty taste of the racket handle. "Let's all go to the five-and-ten and buy a Batmobile."

"Yippee," the small boy said limply, glancing wide-eyed from one of his parents to the other, as if the space between them had gone treacherous.

Richard took the children to the five-and-ten, to the playground, and to a hamburger stand for lunch. These blameless activities transmuted the residue of alcohol and phlegm into a woolly fatigue as pure as the sleep of infants. Obligingly he nodded while his son described a boundless plot: " . . . and then, see Dad, the Penguin had an umbrella smoke came out of, it was neat, and there were these two other guys with funny masks in the bank, filling it with water, I don't know why, to make it bust or something, and Robin was climbing up these slippery stacks of like half-dollars to get away from the water, and then, see Dad . . . "

Back home, the children dispersed into the neighborhood on the same mysterious tide that on other days packed their back yard with unfamiliar urchins. Joan returned from tennis glazed with sweat, her ankles coated with dust. Her body was swimming in the rose afterglow of exertion. He suggested they take a nap.

"Just a nap," she warned.

"Of course," he said. "I met my mistress at the playground and we satisfied each other on the jungle gym."

"Marlene and I beat Alice and Liz. It can't be any of those three, they were waiting for me half an hour."

In bed—the shades strangely drawn against the bright afternoon, a glass of stale water standing bubbled with secret light—he asked her, "You think I want to make you more interesting than you are?"

"Of course. You're bored. You left me and Mack alone deliberately. It was very uncharacteristic of you, to go out with a cold."

"It's sad, to think of you without a lover."

"I'm sorry."

"You're pretty interesting anyway. Here, and here, and here."

"I said really a nap."

In the upstairs hall, on the other side of the closed bedroom door, the telephone rang. After four peals—icy spears hurled from afar—the ringing stopped, unanswered. There was a puzzled pause. Then a tentative, questioning *pring*, as if someone in passing had bumped the table, followed by a determined series, strides of sound, imperative and plaintive, that did not stop until twelve had been counted; then the lover hung up.

Waiting Up

After 9:30, when the last child, Judith, had been tucked into bed with a kiss that, now that she was twelve and as broad-faced as an adult, was frightening in the dark—the baby she had once been suspended at an immense height above the warm-mouthed woman she was becoming—Richard went downstairs and began to wait up for his wife. His mother had always waited up for him and for his father, keeping the house lit against their return from the basketball game, the swimming meet, the midnight adventure with the broken-down car. Entering the house on those nights, in from the cold, the boy had felt his mother as the dazzling center of a stationary, preferable world, and been jealous of her evening alone, in the warmth, with the radio. Now, taking up her old role, he made toast for himself, and drank a glass of milk, and flicked on television, and flicked it off, and poured some bourbon, and found his eyes unable to hold steady upon even a newspaper. He walked to the window and stared out at the street, where an elm not yet dead broke into nervous lace the light of a street lamp. Then he went into the kitchen and stared at the darkness of the backyard where, after a splash of headlights and the sob of a motor being cut, Joan would appear.

When the invitation came, they had agreed she might be out till eleven. But by 10:30 his heart was jarring, the bourbon began to go down as easily as water, and he discovered himself standing in a room with no memory of walking through the doorway. That Picasso plate chosen together in Vallauris. Those college anthologies mingled on the shelves. The battlefield litter of children's schoolbooks and playthings, abandoned in the after-supper rout. At 11:05 he strode to the phone and put his hand on the receiver but was unable to dial the number that lived in his fingers like a musical phrase. Her number. Their number, the Masons'. The house that had swallowed his wife was one where he had always felt comfortable and welcome, a house much like his own, yet different enough in every detail to be exciting, and one whose mistress, waiting in it alone, for him, had stood naked at the head of the stairs. A dazzling welcome, her shoulders caped in morning sun coming through the window, the very filaments of her flesh on fire.

He went upstairs and checked on each sleeping child in the hope that thus a half-hour of waiting would be consumed. Down in the kitchen again he found that only five minutes had passed and, balked from more bourbon by the certainty that he would become drunk, tried to become angry. He thought of smashing the glass, realized that only he was here to clean it up, and set it down empty on the counter. Anger had never been easy for him; even as a child he had seen there was nobody to be angry at, only tired people anxious to please, good hearts asleep and awake, wrapped in the limits of a universe that itself, from the beauty of its details and its contagious air of freedom, seemed to have been well-intentioned. He tried, instead, to pass the time, to cry—but produced only the ridiculous dry snarling tears of a man alone. He might wake the children. He went outdoors, into the back yard. Through bushes that had shed their leaves he watched headlights hurrying home from meetings, from movies, from trysts. He imagined that tonight he would know the lights of her car even before they turned up the alley and flooded the yard in returning. The yard remained dark. The traffic was diminishing. He went back inside. The kitchen clock said 11:35. He went to the telephone and stared at it, puzzled by the problem it presented, of an invisible lock his fingers could not break. Thus he missed Joan's headlights turning into the yard. By the time he looked she was walking toward him, beneath the maple tree, from the deadened car. She was wearing a white coat. He opened the kitchen door to greet her, but his impulse of embrace, to socket her into his chest like a heart that had orbited and returned, was abruptly obsolete, rendered showy and false by his wife's total, disarming familiarity.

He asked, "How was it?"

She groaned. "They were both having terrible times finishing their sentences. It was agony."

"Poor souls. Poor Joan." He remembered his own agony. "You promised to be home by eleven."

In the kitchen she took off her coat and threw it over a chair. "I know, but it would have been too rude to leave, they were both so full of goodness and love. It was *ter*ribly frustrating; they wouldn't let me be angry." Her face looked flushed, her eyes bright, flying past his toward the counter, where the bourbon waited.

"You can be angry at *me,*" he offered.

"I'm too tired. I'm too confused. They were so sweet. He's not angry at you, and she can't imagine why I should be angry at her. Maybe I'm crazy. Could you make me a drink?"

She sat down on the kitchen chair, on top of her coat. "They're like my parents," she said. "They believe in the perfectibility of man."

He gave her the drink, and prompted, "She wouldn't let you be angry."

Joan sipped and sighed; she was like an actress just off the stage, her gestures still imbued with theatrical exaggeration. "I asked her how *she'd* feel and she said she'd have been *pleased* if I'd slept with him, that there isn't any woman she'd rather he slept with, that I would have been a gift she'd have given out of *love*. She kept calling me her best friend, on and on in that soothing steady voice; I'd never thought of her as *that* much my best friend. All year I'd felt this constraint between us and of course now I know why. All year she's been dancing up to me with this little impish arrogance I couldn't understand."

"She likes you very much and we talked a lot about your reaction. She dreaded it."

"She kept *tell*ing me to be angry with her and of course her telling made it impossible. That soothing steady voice. I don't think she heard a thing I said.

I could see her concentrating, you know, really *con*centrating, on my lips, but all the time she was framing what she was going to say next. She's been working on those speeches for a year. I'm looped. *Don't* give me any more bourbon."

"And he?"

"Oh, he. He was crazy. He kept talking of it as a *revelation*. Apparently they've been having great sex ever since she told him. He kept using words like understanding and compassion and how we must all *help* each other. It was like church, and you know how agitated I get in church, how I begin to cry. Every time I'd try to cry he'd kiss me, then he'd kiss her: absolutely impartial. Peck, peck. We're the same person! She's stolen my identity!" She held up her glass of ice cubes and raised her eyebrows in indignation. Her hair, too, seemed to be lifting from her scalp; she had once described to him how at golf, when she flubbed a shot, she could hear her hair rustle as it rose in fury.

"You have bushier hair," he said.

"Thanks. You're the one to know. He kept wanting to call you up. He kept saying things like, 'Let's get good old Richard down here, the son of a bitch. I miss the old seducer.' I had to keep telling him we needed you to baby-sit."

"Pretty unmanning."

"I think you've had enough manning for a while."

"You should have seen me waiting up. I kept running to all the windows like a hen with a lost chick. I was frantic for you, sweet. I never should have sent you down to those awful people to be lectured at."

"They're not awful people. *You're* the awful person. You're just lucky they don't believe in war. They think indignation is silly. Childish. They're so ex*plan*atory, is all. He kept talking about some greater good coming out of this."

"And you? You believe in war, or a greater good?"

"I don't know. I could believe in a little more bourbon."

His next question was hot, so full of remembered light it scorched his tongue. "Did she also want me there?"

"She didn't say. She's not *that* tactless."

"I never found her tactless," he dared say.

Joan's hair appeared to puff out from her head; she gestured like a soprano. "Why didn't you run off with her? Why don't you run off with her now? *Do* something. I can't *stand* another one of these love-ins, or teach-ins, or whatever they are. They kept saying, we must all get together, we must all keep in touch. I don't want to get together with *any*body."

"But it's you—" he began.

She interrupted: "Don't spare the ice."

"—I seem to want most. I hated your being out of the house tonight. I hated it more than I would have supposed." He spoke very carefully, gazing downward at the counter as he refilled their glasses, which seemed balanced on the edge of a precipice; Joan's safe return had uncovered within him the abysmal loss of, with her soothing steady voice, the other.

Eros Rampant

The Maples' house is full of love. Bean, the six-year-old baby, loves Hecuba, the dog. John, who is eight, an angel-faced mystic serenely unable to ride a bicycle or read a clock, is in love with his Creepy Crawlers, his monster cards, his dinosaurs, and his carved rhinoceros from Kenya. He spends hours in his room after school drifting among these things, rearranging, gloating, humming. He experiences pain only when his older brother, Richard Jr., sardonically enters his room and pierces his placenta of contemplation. Richard is in love with life, with all outdoors, with Carl Yastrzemski, Babe Parelli, the Boston Bruins, the Beatles, and with that shifty apparition who, comb in hand, peeps back shiny-eyed at him out of the mirror in the mornings, wearing a mustache of toothpaste. He receives strange challenging notes from girls—*Dickie Maple you stop looking at me*—which he brings home from school carelessly crumpled along with his spelling papers and hectographed notices about eye, tooth, and lung inspection. His feelings about young Mrs. Brice, who confronts his section of the fifth grade with the enameled poise and studio diction of an airline hostess, are so guarded as to be suspicious. He almost certainly loves, has always deeply loved, his older sister, Judith. Verging on thirteen, she has become difficult to contain, even within an incestuous passion. Large and bumptious, she eclipses his view of the television screen, loudly Frugs while he would listen to the Beatles, teases, thrashes, is bombarded and jogged by powerful rays from outer space. She hangs for hours by the corner where Mr. Lunt, her history teacher, lives; she pastes effigies of the Monkees on her walls, French-kisses her mother goodnight, experiences the panic of sleeplessness, engages in long languorous tussles on the sofa with the dog. Hecuba, a spayed golden retriever, races from room to room, tormented as if by fleas by the itch for adoration, ears flattened, tail thumping, until at last she runs up against the cats, who do not love her, and she drops exhausted, in grateful defeat, on the kitchen linoleum, and sleeps. The cats, Esther and Esau, lick each other's fur and share a bowl. They had been two of a litter. Esther, the mother of more than thirty kittens mostly resembling her brother, but with a persistent black minority vindicating the howled appeal of a neighboring tom, has been "fixed"; Esau, sentimentally allowed to continue unfixed, now must venture from the house in quest of the bliss that had once been purely domestic. He returns scratched and battered. Esther licks his wounds while he leans dazed beside the refrigerator; even his purr is ragged. Nagging for their supper, they sit like bookends, their backs discreetly touching, an expert old married couple on the dole. One feels, unexpectedly, that Esau still loves Esther, while she merely accepts and understands him. She seems scornful of his merely dutiful attentions. Is she puzzled by her abrupt surgical lack of what drastically attracts him? But it is his big square tomcat's head that seems puzzled, rather than her triangular feminine feline one. The children feel a difference; both Bean and John cuddle Esau more, now that Esther is sterile. Perhaps, obscurely, they feel that she has deprived them of a miracle, of the semiannual miracle of her kittens, of drowned miniature piglets wriggling alive from a black orifice vaster than a cave. Richard Jr., as if to demonstrate his superior purchase on manhood and its righteous compassion, makes a point of petting the two cats equally, stroke for stroke. Judith claims she hates them both; it is her chore to feed them supper, and she hates the smell of horsemeat. She loves, at least in the abstract, horses.

Mr. Maple loves Mrs. Maple. He goes through troublesome periods, often on Saturday afternoons, of being unable to take his eyes from her, of being captive to the absurd persuasion that the curve of her solid haunch conceals, enwraps, a precarious treasure confided to his care. He cannot touch her enough. The sight of her body contorted by one of her yoga exercises, in her elastic black leotard riddled with runs, twists his heart so that he cannot breathe. Her gesture as she tips the dregs of white wine into a potted geranium seems infinite, like one of Vermeer's moments frozen in an eternal light from the left. At night he tries to press her into himself, to secure her drowsy body against his breast like a clasp, as if without it he will come undone. He cannot sleep in this position, yet maintains it long after her breathing has become steady and oblivious: can love be defined, simply, as the refusal to sleep? Also he loves Penelope Vogel, a quaint little secretary at his office who is recovering from a disastrous affair with an Antiguan; and he is in love with the memories of six or so other women, beginning with a seven-year-old playmate who used to steal his hunter's cap; and is half in love with death. He as well seems to love, perhaps alone in the nation, President Johnson, who is unaware of his existence. Along the same lines, Richard adores the moon; he studies avidly all the photographs beamed back from its uncongenial surface.

And Joan? Whom does she love? Her psychiatrist, certainly. Her father, inevitably. Her yoga instructor, probably. She has a part-time job in a museum and returns home flushed and quick-tongued, as if from sex. She must love the children, for they flock to her like sparrows to suet. They fight bitterly for a piece of her lap and turn their backs upon their father, as if he, the source and shelter of their life, were a grotesque intruder, a chimney sweep in a snow palace. None of his impersonations with the children—scoutmaster, playmate, confidant, financial bastion, factual wizard, watchman of the night—win them over; Bean still cries for Mommy when hurt, John approaches her for the money to finance yet more monster cards, Dickie demands that hers be the last goodnight, and even Judith, who should be his, kisses him timidly, and saves her open-mouthed passion for her mother. Joan swims through their love like a fish through water, ignorant of any other element. Love slows her footsteps, pours upon her from the radio, hangs about her, in the kitchen, in the form of tacked-up children's drawings of houses, families, cars, cats, dogs, and flowers. Her husband cannot touch her: she is solid but hidden, like the World Bank; presiding yet immaterial, like the federal judiciary. Some cold uncoördinated thing pushes at his hand as it hangs impotent; it is Hecuba's nose. Obese spayed golden-eyed bitch, like him she abhors exclusion and strains to add her warmth to the tumble, in love with them all, in love with the smell of food, in love with the smell of love.

Penelope Vogel takes care to speak without sentimentality; five years younger than Richard, she has endured a decade of amorous ordeals and, still single at twenty-nine, preserves herself by speaking dryly, in the flip phrases of a still younger generation.

"We had a good thing," she says of her Antiguan, "that became a bad scene."

She handles, verbally, her old affairs like dried flowers; sitting across the restaurant table from her, Richard is made jittery by her delicacy, as if he and a grandmother are together examining an array of brittle, enigmatic mementos. "A very undesirable scene," Penelope adds. "The big time was too much for him. He got in with the drugs crowd. I couldn't see it."

"He wanted to marry you?" Richard asks timidly; this much is office gossip.

She shrugs, admitting, "There was that pitch."

"You must miss him."

"There is that. He was the most beautiful man I ever saw. His shoulders. In Dickinson's Bay, he'd have me put my hand on his shoulder in the water and that way he'd pull me along for miles, swimming. He was a snorkel instructor."

"His name?" Jittery, fearful of jarring these reminiscences, which are also negotiations, he spills the last of his Gibson, and jerkily signals to order another.

"Hubert," Penelope says. She is patiently mopping with her napkin. "Like a girl friend told me, Never take on a male beauty, you'll have to fight for the mirror." Her face is small and very white, and her nose very long, her pink nostrils inflamed by a perpetual cold. Only a Negro, Richard thinks, could find her beautiful; the thought gives her, in the restless shadowy restaurant light, beauty. The waiter, colored, comes and changes their tablecloth. Penelope continues so softly Richard must strain to hear, "When Hubert was eighteen he had a woman divorce her husband and leave her children for him. She was one of the old planter families. He wouldn't marry her. He told me, If she'd do that to him, next thing she'd leave me. He was very moralistic, until he came up here. But imagine an eighteen-year-old boy having an effect like that on a mature married woman in her thirties."

"I better keep him away from my wife," Richard jokes.

"Yeah." She does not smile. "They *work* at it, you know. Those boys are *pros*."

Penelope has often been to the West Indies. In St. Croix, it delicately emerges, there was Andrew, with his goatee and his septic-tank business and his political ambitions; in Guadeloupe, there was Ramon, a customs inspector; in Trinidad, Castlereigh, who played the alto pans in a steel band and also did the limbo. He could go down to nine inches. But Hubert was the worst, or best. He was the only one who had followed her north. "I was supposed to come live with him in this hotel in Dorchester but I was scared to go near the place, full of cop-out types and the smell of pot in the elevator, I got two offers from guys just standing there pushing the Up button. It was not a healthy scene." The waiter brings them rolls; in his shadow her profile seems wan and he yearns to pluck her, pale flower, from the tangle she had conjured. "It got so bad," she says, "I tried going back to an old boy friend, an awfully nice guy with a mother and a nervous stomach. He's a computer systems analyst, very dedicated, but I don't know, he just never impressed me. All he can talk about is his gastritis and how she keeps telling him to move out and get a wife, but he doesn't know if she means it. His mother."

"He is . . . white?"

Penelope glances up; there is a glint off her halted butter knife. Her voice slows, goes drier. "No, as a matter of fact. He's what they call an Afro-American. You mind?"

"No, no, I was just wondering—his nervous stomach. He doesn't sound like the others."

"He's not. Like I say, he doesn't impress me. Don't you find, once you have something that works, it's hard to back up?" More seems meant than is stated; her level gaze, as she munches her thickly buttered bun, feels like one tangent in a complicated geometrical problem: find the point at which she had switched from white to black lovers.

The subject is changed for him; his heart jars, and he leans forward hastily to say, "See that woman who just came in? Leather suit, gypsy earrings, sitting down now? Her name is Eleanor Dennis. She lives down our street from us. She's divorced."

"Who's the man?"

"I have no idea. Eleanor's moved out of our

circles. He looks like a real thug." Along the far wall, Eleanor adjusts the great loop of her earring; her sideways glance, in the shuffle of shadows, flicks past his table. He doubts that she saw him.

Penelope says, "From the look on your face, that was more than a circle she was in with you."

He pretends to be disarmed by her guess, but in truth considers it providential that one of his own old loves should appear, to countervail the dark torrent of hers. For the rest of the meal they talk about *him*, him and Eleanor and Marlene Brossman and Joan and the little girl who used to steal his hunter's cap. In the lobby of Penelope's apartment house, the elevator summoned, he offers to go up with her.

She says carefully, "I don't think you want to."

"But I *do*." The building is Back Bay modern; the lobby is garishly lit and furnished with plastic plants that need never be watered, Naugahyde chairs that were never sat upon, and tessellated plaques no one ever looks at. The light is an absolute presence, as even and clean as the light inside a freezer, as ubiquitous as ether or as the libido that, Freud says, permeates us all from infancy on.

"No," Penelope repeats. "I've developed a good ear for sincerity in these things, I think you're too wrapped up back home."

"The dog likes me," he confesses, and kisses her

goodnight there, encased in brightness. Dry voice to the contrary, her lips are shockingly soft, wide, warm, and sorrowing.

"So," Joan says to him. "You slept with that little office mouse." It is Saturday; the formless erotic suspense of the afternoon—the tennis games, the cartoon matinees—has passed. The Maples are in their room dressing for a party, by the ashen light of dusk, and the watery blue of a distant street lamp.

"I never have," he says, thereby admitting, however, that he knows who she means.

"Well you took her to dinner."

"Who says?"

"Mack Dennis. Eleanor saw the two of you in a restaurant."

"When do they converse? I thought they were divorced."

"They talk all the time. He's still in love with her. Everybody knows that."

"O.K. When do he and *you* converse?"

Oddly, she has not prepared an answer. "Oh—" His heart falls through her silence. "Maybe I saw him in the hardware store this afternoon."

"And maybe you didn't. Why would he blurt this out anyway? You and he must be on cozy terms."

He says this to trigger her denial; but she mutely

considers and, sauntering toward her closet, admits, "We understand each other."

How unlike her, to bluff this way. "When was I supposedly seen?"

"You mean it happens often? Last Wednesday, around eight-thirty. You *must* have slept with her."

"I couldn't have. I was home by ten, you may remember. You had just gotten back yourself from the museum."

"What went wrong, darley? Did you offend her with your horrible pro-Vietnam stand?"

In the dim light he hardly knows this woman, her broken gestures, her hasty voice. Her silver slip glows and crackles as she wriggles into a black knit cocktail dress; with a kind of determined agitation she paces around the bed, to the bureau and back. As she moves, her body seems to be gathering bulk from the shadows, bulk and a dynamic elasticity. He tries to placate her with a token offering of truth. "No, it turns out Penelope only goes with Negroes. I'm too pale for her."

"You admit you tried?"

He nods.

"Well," Joan says, and takes a half-step toward him, so that he flinches in anticipation of being hit, "do you want to know who *I* was sleeping with Wednesday?"

He nods again, but the two nods feel different,

as if, transposed by a terrific unfelt speed, a continent had lapsed between them.

She names a man he knows only slightly, an assistant director in the museum, who wears a collar pin and has his gray hair cut long and tucked back in the foppish English style. "It was *fun,*" Joan says, kicking at a shoe. "He thinks I'm *beau*tiful. He cares for me in a way you just *don't.*" She kicks away the other shoe. "You look pale to me too, buster."

Stunned, he needs to laugh. "But we *all* think you're beautiful."

"Well you don't make me *feel* it."

"*I* feel it," he says.

"You make me feel like an ugly drudge." As they grope to understand their new positions, they realize that she, like a chess player who has impulsively swept forward her queen, has nowhere to go but on the defensive. In a desperate attempt to keep the initiative, she says, "Divorce me. Beat me."

He is calm, factual, admirable. "How often have you been with him?"

"I don't know. Since April, off and on." Her hands appear to embarrass her; she places them at her sides, against her cheeks, together on the bedpost, off. "I've been trying to get out of it, I've felt horribly guilty, but he's never been at all pushy, so

I could never really arrange a fight. He gets this hurt look."

"Do you want to keep him?"

"With you knowing? Don't be grotesque."

"But he cares for you in a way I just don't."

"Any lover does that."

"God help us. You're an expert."

"Hardly."

"What *about* you and Mack?"

She is frightened. "Years ago. Not for very long."

"And Freddy Vetter?"

"No, we agreed not. He knew about me and Mack."

Love, a cloudy heavy ink, inundates him from within, suffuses his palms with tingling pressure as he steps close to her, her murky face held tense against the expectation of a blow. "You whore," he breathes, enraptured. "My virgin bride." He kisses her hands; they are corrupt and cold. "Who else?" he begs, as if each name is a burden of treasure she lays upon his bowed serf's shoulders. "Tell me all your men."

"I've told you. It's a pretty austere list. You know *why* I told you? So you wouldn't feel guilty about this Vogel person."

"But nothing happened. When you do it, it happens."

"Sweetie, I'm a woman," she explains, and they do seem, in this darkening room above the muted hubbub of television, to have reverted to the bases of their marriage, to the elemental constituents. Woman. Man. House.

"What does your psychiatrist say about all this?"

"Not much." The triumphant swell of her confession has passed; her ebbed manner prepares for days, weeks of his questions. She retrieves the shoes she kicked away. "That's one of the reasons I went to him, I kept having these affairs—"

"*Kept* having? You're killing me."

"Please don't interrupt. It was somehow very innocent. I'd go into his office, and lie down, and say, 'I've just been with Mack, or Otto—' "

"Otto. What's that joke? Otto spelled backwards is 'Otto.' Otto spelled inside out is 'toot.' "

"—and I'd say it was wonderful, or awful, or so-so, and then we'd talk about my childhood masturbation. It's not his business to scold me, it's his job to get me to stop scolding myself."

"The poor bastard, all the time I've been jealous of *him*, and he's been suffering with this for years; he had to listen every *day*. You'd go in there and plunk yourself still warm down on his couch—"

"It wasn't every day at all. Weeks would go by. I'm not Otto's only woman."

The artificial tumult of television below merges with a real commotion, a screaming and bumping that mounts the stairs and threatens the aquarium where the Maples are swimming, dark fish in ink, their outlines barely visible, known to each other only as eddies of warmth, as mysterious animate chasms in the surface of space. Fearing that for years he will not again be so close to Joan, or she be so open, he hurriedly asks, "And what about the yoga instructor?"

"Don't be silly," Joan says, clasping her pearls at the nape of her neck. "He's an elderly vegetarian."

The door crashes open; their bedroom explodes in shards of electric light. Richard Jr. is frantic, sobbing.

"Mommy, Judy keeps *teasing* me and getting in front of the *tele*vision!"

"I did not. I did not." Judith speaks very distinctly. "Mother and Father, he is a retarded liar."

"She can't help she's growing," Richard tells his son, picturing poor Judith trying to fit herself among the intent childish silhouettes in the little television room, pitying her for her size, much as he pities Johnson for his Presidency. Bean bursts into the bedroom, frightened by violence not on TV, and Hecuba leaps upon the bed with rolling golden eyes, and Judith gives Dickie an impudent and unrepentant sideways glance, and he, gagging on a surfeit of emotion, bolts from the room. Soon there arises from the other end of the upstairs an anguished squawk as Dickie invades John's room and punctures his communion with his dinosaurs.

Downstairs, a woman, neglected and alone, locked in a box, sings about *amore*. Bean hugs Joan's legs so she cannot move.

Judith asks with parental sharpness, "What were you two talking about?"

"Nothing," Richard says. "We were getting dressed."

"Why were all the lights out?"

"We were saving electricity," her father tells her.

"Why is Mommy crying?" He looks, disbelieving, and discovers that indeed, her cheeks coated with silver, she is.

At the party, amid clouds of friends and smoke, Richard resists being parted from his wife's side. She has dried her tears, and faintly swaggers, as when, on the beach, she dares wear a bikini. But her nakedness is only in his eyes. Her head beside his shoulder, her grave polite pleasantries, the plump unrepentant cleft between her breasts, all seem newly treasurable and intrinsic to his own identity. As a cuckold, he has grown taller, attenuated, more elegant and humane in his opinions, airier and more mobile. When the usual argument about Vietnam commences, he hears himself sounding like a dove. He concedes that Johnson is unlovable. He allows that Asia is infinitely complex, devious, ungrateful, feminine: but must we abandon her therefore? When Mack Dennis, grown burly in bachelorhood, comes and asks Joan to dance, Richard feels unmanned and sits on the sofa with such an air of weariness that Marlene Brossman sits down beside him and, for the first time in years, flirts. He tries to tell her with his voice, beneath the meaningless words he is speaking, that he loved her, and could love her again, but that at the moment he is terribly distracted and must be excused. He goes and asks Joan if it isn't time to go. She resists: "It's too rude." She is safe here among proprieties and foresees that his exploitation of the territory she has surrendered will be thorough. Love is pitiless. They drive home at midnight under a slim moon nothing like its photographs—shadow-caped canyons, gimlet mountain ranges, gritty circular depressions around the metal feet of the mechanical intruder sent from the blue ball in the sky.

They do not rest until he has elicited from her a world of details: dates, sites, motel interiors, precisely mixed emotions. They make love, self-critically. He exacts the new wantonness she owes him, and in compensation tries to be, like a battered old roué, skillful. He satisfies himself that in some elemental way he has never been displaced; that for months she has been struggling in her lover's grasp, in the gauze net of love, her wings pinioned by tact. She assures him that she seized on the first opportunity for confession; she confides to him that Otto spray-sets his hair and uses perfume. She, weeping, vows that nowhere, never, has she encountered his, Richard's, passion, his pleasant bodily proportions and backwards-reeling grace, his invigorating sadism, his male richness. Then why . . . ? She is asleep. Her breathing has become oblivious. He clasps her limp body to his, wasting forgiveness upon her ghostly form. A receding truck pulls the night's silence taut. She has left him a hair short of satiety; her confession feels still a fraction unplumbed. The lunar face of the electric clock says three. He turns, flips his pillow, restlessly adjusts his arms, turns again, and seems to go downstairs for a glass of milk.

To his surprise, the kitchen is brightly lit, and Joan is on the linoleum floor, in her leotard. He stands amazed while she serenely twists her legs into the lotus position. He asks her again about the yoga instructor.

"Well, I didn't think it counted if it was part of the exercise. The whole point, darley, is to make mind and body one. This is Pranayama—breath control." Stately, she pinches shut one nostril and slowly inhales, then pinches shut the other and exhales. Her hands return, palm up, to her knees. And she smiles. "This one is fun. It's called the Twist." She assumes a new position, her muscles elastic under the black cloth tormented into runs. "Oh, I forgot to tell you, I've slept with Harry Saxon."

"Joan, no. How often?"

"When we felt like it. We used to go out behind the Little League field. That heavenly smell of clover."

"But sweetie, why?"

Smiling, she inwardly counts the seconds of this position. "You know why. He asked. It's hard, when men ask. You mustn't insult their male natures. There's a harmony in everything."

"And Freddy Vetter? You lied about Freddy, didn't you?"

"Now *this* pose is wonderful for the throat muscles. It's called the Lion. You mustn't laugh." She kneels, her buttocks on her heels, and tilts back her head, and from gaping jaws thrusts out her tongue as if to touch the ceiling. Yet she continues speaking. "The whole theory is, we hold our heads too high, and blood can't get to the brain."

His chest hurts; he forces from it the cry, "Tell me everybody!"

She rolls toward him and stands upright on her shoulders, her face flushed with the effort of equilibrium and the downflow of blood. Her legs slowly scissor open and shut. "Some men you don't know," she goes on. "They come to the door to sell you septic tanks." Her voice is coming from her belly. Worse, there is a humming. Terrified, he awakes, and sits up. His chest is soaked.

He locates the humming as a noise from the transformer on the telephone pole near their windows. All night, while its residents sleep, the town communes with itself electrically. Richard's terror persists, generating mass as the reality of his dream sensations is confirmed. Joan's body seems small, scarcely bigger than Judith's, and narrower with age, yet infinitely deep, an abyss of secrecy, perfidy, and acceptingness; acrophobia launches sweat from his palms. He leaves the bed as if scrambling backward from the lip of a vortex. He again goes downstairs; his wife's revelations have steepened the treads and left the walls slippery.

The kitchen is dark; he turns on the light. The floor is bare. The familiar objects of the kitchen seem discovered in a preservative state of staleness, wearing a look of tension, as if they are about to burst with the strain of being so faithfully themselves. Esther and Esau pad in from the living room, where they have been sleeping on the sofa, and beg to be fed, sitting like bookends, expectant and expert. The clock says four. Watchman of the night. But in searching for signs of criminal entry, for traces of his dream, Richard finds nothing but—clues mocking in their very abundance—the tacked-up drawings done by children's fingers ardently bunched around a crayon, of houses, cars, cats, and flowers.

Plumbing

The old plumber bends forward tenderly, in the dusk of the cellar of my new house, to show me a precious, antique joint. "They haven't done them like this for thirty years," he tells me. His thin voice is like a trickle squeezed through rust. "Thirty, forty years. When I began with my father, we did them like this. It's an old lead joint. You wiped it on. You poured it hot with a ladle and held a wet rag in the other hand. There were sixteen motions you had to make before it cooled. Sixteen distinct motions. Otherwise you lost it and ruined the joint.

You had to chip it away and begin again. That's how we had to do it when I started out. A boy of maybe fifteen, sixteen. This joint here could be fifty years old."

He knows my plumbing; I merely own it. He has known it through many owners. We think we are what we think and see when in truth we are upright bags of tripe. We think we have bought living space and a view when in truth we have bought a maze, a history, an archaeology of pipes and cut-ins and traps and valves. The plumber shows me some stout dark pipe that follows a diagonal course into the foundation wall. "See that line along the bottom there?" A line of white, a whisper of frosting on the dark pipe's underside —pallid oxidation. "Don't touch it. It'll start to bleed. See, they cast this old soil pipe in two halves. They were supposed to mount them so the seams were on the sides. But sometimes they mounted them so the seam is on the bottom." He demonstrates with cupped hands; his hands part so the crack between them widens. I strain to see between his dark palms and become by his metaphor water seeking the light. "Eventually, see, it leaks."

With his flashlight beam he follows the telltale pale line backward. "Four, five new sections should do it." He sighs, wheezes; his eyes open wider than other men's, from a life spent in the dusk. He is a poet. Where I see only a flaw, a vexing imperfection that will cost me money, he gazes fondly, musing upon the eternal presences of corrosion and flow. He sends me magnificent ironical bills, wherein catalogues of tiny parts—

1	1¼ x 1″ galv bushing	58¢
1	⅜″ brass pet cock	90¢
3	½″ blk nipple	23¢

—itemized with an accountancy so painstaking as to seem mad are in the end offset and swallowed by a torrential round figure attributed merely to "Labor":

Labor $550.

I suppose that his tender meditations with me now, even the long pauses when his large eyes blink, are Labor.

The old house, the house we left, a mile away, seems relieved to be rid of our furniture. The rooms where we lived, where we staged our meals and ceremonies and self-dramatizations and where some of us went from infancy to adolescence, rooms and stairways so imbued with our daily motions that their irregularities were bred into our bones and could be traversed in the dark, do not seem to mourn, as I had thought they would. The house exults in its sudden size, in the reach of its empty corners. Floorboards long muffled by carpets shine as if freshly varnished. Sun pours unobstructed through the curtainless windows. The house is young again. It, too, had a self, a life, which for a time was eclipsed by our lives; now, before its new owners come to burden it, it is free. Now only moonlight makes the floor creak. When, some mornings, I return, to retrieve a few final oddments—andirons, picture frames—the space of the house greets me with a virginal impudence. Opening the front door is like opening the door to the cat who comes in with the morning milk, who mews in passing on his way to the beds still warm with our night's sleep, his routine so tenuously attached to ours, by a single mew and a shared roof. Nature is tougher than ecologists admit. Our house forgot us in a day.

I feel guilty that we occupied it so thinly, that a trio of movers and a day's breezes could so completely clean us out. When we moved in, a dozen years ago, I was surprised that the house, though its beams and fireplaces were three hundred years old, was not haunted. I had thought, it being so old, it would be. But an amateur witch my wife had known at college tapped the bedroom walls, sniffed the attic, and assured us—like my plumber, come to think of it, she had unnaturally distended eyes—that the place was clean. Puritan hayfarmers had built it. In the nineteenth century, it may have served as a tavern; the pike to Newburyport ran right by. In the 1930s, it had been a tenement, the rooms now so exultantly large then subdivided by plasterboard partitions that holes were poked through, so the tenants could trade sugar and flour. Rural days, poor days. Chickens had been kept upstairs for a time; my children at first said that when it rained they could smell feathers, but I took this to be the power of suggestion, a myth. Digging in the back yard, we did unearth some pewter spoons and chunks of glass bottles from a lost era of packaging. Of ourselves, a few plastic practice golf balls in the iris and a few dusty little Superballs beneath the radiators will be all for others to find. The ghosts we have left only we can see.

I see a man in a tuxedo and a woman in a long white dress stepping around the back yard, in a cold drizzle that makes them laugh, at two o'clock on Easter morning. They are hiding chocolate eggs in tinfoil and are drunk. In the morning, they will have sickly-sweet headaches, and children will wake them with the shrieks and quarrels of the hunt, and come to their parents' bed with chocolate-smeared mouths and sickening sweet breaths; but it is the apparition of early morning I see, from the perspective of a sober conscience standing in the kitchen, these two partygoers tiptoeing in the muddy yard, around the forsythia bush, up to the swing set and back. Easter bunnies.

A man bends above a child's bed; his voice and a child's voice murmur prayers in unison. They have trouble with "trespasses" versus "debts," having attended different Sunday schools. Weary, slightly asthmatic (the ghost of chicken feathers?), anxious to return downstairs to a book and a drink, he passes into the next room. The child there, a bigger child, when he offers to bow his head with her, cries softly, "Daddy, no, don't!" The round white face, dim in the dusk of the evening, seems to glow with tension, embarrassment, appeal. Embarrassed himself, too easily embarrassed, he gives her a kiss, backs off, closes her bedroom door, leaves her to the darkness.

In the largest room, its walls now bare but for phantasmal rectangles where bookcases stood and pictures hung, people are talking, gesturing dramatically. The woman, the wife, throws something —it had been about to be an ashtray, but even in her fury, which makes her face rose-red, she prudently switched to a book. She bursts into tears, perhaps at her Puritan inability to throw the ashtray, and runs into another room, not forgetting to hop over the little raised threshold where strangers to the house often trip. Children sneak quietly up and down the stairs, pale, guilty, blaming themselves, in the vaults of their innocent hearts, for this disruption. Even the dog curls her tail under, ashamed. The man sits slumped on a sofa that is no longer there. His ankles are together, his head is bowed, as if shackles restrict him. He is dramatizing his conception of himself, as a prisoner. It seems to be summer, for a little cabbage butterfly irrelevantly alights on the window screen, where hollyhocks rub and tap. The woman returns, pink in the face instead of red, and states matters in a formal, deliberated way; the man stands and shouts. She hits him; he knocks her arm away and punches her side, startled by how pleasant, how spongy, the sensation is. A sack of guts. They flounce among the furniture, which gets in their way, releasing whiffs of dust. The children edge one step higher on the stairs. The dog, hunched as if being whipped, goes to the screen door and begs to be let out. The man embraces the woman and murmurs. She is pink and warm with tears. He discovers himself weeping; what a good feeling it is!—like vomiting, like sweat. What are they saying, what are these violent, frightened people discussing? They are discussing change, natural process, the passage of time, death.

Feeble ghosts. They fade like breath on glass. In contrast I remember the potent, powerful, numinous Easter eggs of my childhood, filled solid with moist coconut, heavy as ingots, or else capacious like theatres, populated by paper silhouettes—miniature worlds generating their own sunlight. These eggs arose, in their nest of purple excelsior, that certain Sunday morning, from the same impossible-to-plumb well of mystery where the stars swarm, and old photographs predating my birth were snapped, and God listened. At night, praying, I lay like a needle on the surface of this abyss, in a house haunted to the shadowy corners by Disneyesque menaces with clutching fingernails, in a town that boasted a funeral parlor at its main intersection and that was ringed all around its outskirts by barns blazoned with Jesus signs. On the front-parlor rug was a continent-shaped stain where as a baby I had vomited. Myth upon myth: now I am three or four, a hungry soul, eating dirt from one of the large parlor pots that hold strange ferns—feathery, cloudy, tropical presences. One of my grandmother's superstitions is that a child must eat a pound of dirt a year to grow strong. And then later, at nine or ten, I am lying on my belly, in the same spot, reading the newspaper to my blind grandfather—first the obituaries, then the rural news, and lastly the front-page headlines about Japs and Roosevelt. The paper has a deep smell, not dank like the smell of comic books but fresher, less sweet than doughnut bags but spicy, an exciting smell that has the future in it, a smell of things stacked and crisp and faintly warm, the smell of the *new*. Each day, I realize, this smell arrives and fades. And then I am thirteen and saying goodbye to the front parlor. We are moving. Beside the continent-shaped stain on the carpet are the round stains of the fern flower-pots. The uncurtained sunlight on these stains is a revelation. They are stamped deep, like dinosaur footprints.

Did my children sense the frivolity of our Easter priesthoods? The youngest used to lie in her bed in the smallest of the upstairs rooms and suck her thumb and stare past me at something in the dark. Our house, in her, did surely possess the dimension of dread that imprints every surface on the memory, that makes each scar on the paint a clue to some terrible depth. She was the only child who would talk about death. Tomorrow was her birthday. "I don't want to have a birthday. I don't want to be nine."

"But you must grow. Everybody grows. The trees grow."

"I don't want to."

"Don't you want to be a big girl like Judith?"

"No."

"Then you can wear lipstick, and a bra, and ride your bicycle even on Central Street."

"I don't want to ride on Central Street."

"Why not?"

"Because then I will get to be an old old lady and die."

And her tears well up, and the man with her is dumb, as all the men ever with her will be on this point dumb, in this little room where nothing remains of us but scuff marks and a half-scraped Snoopy decal on the window frame. If we still lived here, it would be time to put the screens in the windows.

Crocuses are up at the old house; daffodils bloom at the new. The children who lived here before us left Superballs under the radiators for us to find. In the days of appraisal and purchase, we used to glimpse these children skulking around their house, behind bushes and banisters, gazing at us, the usurpers of their future. In the days after they moved out but before our furniture moved in, we played hilarious games in the empty rooms—huge comic ricochets and bounces. Soon the balls became lost again. The rooms became crowded.

Tenderly, musingly, the plumber shows me a sawed-off section of the pipe that leads from the well to our pressure tank. The inside diameter of the pipe is reduced to the size of his finger by mineral accretions—a circle of stony layers thin as paper. It suggests a book seen endwise, but one of those books not meant to be opened, that priests wisely kept locked. "See," he says, "this has built up over forty, fifty years. I remember my dad and me putting in the pump, but this pipe was here then. Nothing you can do about it, minerals in the water. Nothing you can do about it but dig it up and replace it with inch-and-a-quarter, inch-and-a-half new."

I imagine my lawn torn up, the great golden backhoe trampling my daffodils, my dollars flooding away. Ineffectually, I protest.

The plumber sighs, as poets do, with an eye on the audience. "See, keep on with it like this, you'll burn out your new pump. It has to work too hard to draw the water. Replace it now, you'll never have to worry with it again. It'll outlast your time here."

My time, his time. His eyes open wide in the unspeaking presences of corrosion and flow. We push out through the bulkhead; a blinding piece of sky slides into place above us, fitted with temporary, timeless clouds. All around us, we are outlasted.

The Red-Herring Theory

The party was over. Their friends had come, shuffled themselves, been reshuffled, worn thin with the evening and then, papery post-midnight presences, had conjured themselves out the door. The Maples were left with each other and a profusion of cigarette butts and emptyish glasses. The dishes were stacked dirty in the kitchen, the children slept in innocence upstairs. Still, the couple, with the hysterical after-energy of duty done, refused to go to bed but instead sat in a living room grown suddenly hollow and huge.

"What messy people," Joan said, perched upright in a director's chair of natural wood and green canvas. "Grinding Fritos into a shag rug. They're so *sloppy.*" Richard saw that she was in a judgmental mood; her pronouncements, when she was in this mood, fascinated him.

"Isn't that how *we* act," he asked, sprawled on the off-white sofa, its pillows battered by a succcession of bodies, "when we go out?" The seats they had chosen placed Joan higher, and displayed to his view the admirable clean line of her jaw.

"Not at all," she said positively. "We clean up what we spill. We always leave together, too."

"That *was* odd," Richard agreed. "Do you think Jim was sick, or mad?"

"Maybe he was so mad it made him sick."

"Was he mad at *me?*"

"Well," Joan said, "you *did* keep dancing with her, even after he put on his overcoat."

"Surely a suburban man," was the languid reply of her husband, who in his adolescence had seen a number of Mr. and Mrs. North movies, "has the right to dance with his mistress."

Joan's reply was enviably firm: "Marlene is not your mistress. She's your red herring."

"My red herring?" The unforeseen phrase tinted Marlene's skin exotically; again, she was in his arms, but slipperier, a mermaid, a scaly smelly merperson. She had been loaded to the gills with perfume.

"Sure," Joan said. "The properly equipped suburban man, as you call him, has a wife, a mistress, and a red herring. The red herring may have been his mistress once, or she may become one in the future, but he's not sleeping with her now. You can tell, because in public they act as though they do."

Richard leaned into another depressed pillow, protesting, "That's too Machiavellian to be real. That's decadent, sweetie. Maybe it was a mistake, to bring you out here; we should have stayed on West Thirteenth Street. Remember how the policemen used to gallop by on horses in the snow?"

"They did that once. Fifteen years ago. The schools were impossible. You couldn't park the car."

"Jesus," he agreed, "remember the time I parked it in a lot and a roof-mending job on the building next to it spilled tar all over the windshield? It still makes me furious." But remembering it made him happy.

"There you are," Joan agreed, "we're stuck," meaning the suburbs. "Want a little nightcap?"

"My God, no. How can you stand any more liquor? Do you think I should call Jim up and apologize?"

"Don't be silly. You might interrupt something."

"I might?" His perfumed merperson, descaled, in another's arms? The thought was chilly.

"It's possible. Marlene didn't seem at all fazed when he went out, she went right on being the life of the party."

Richard shifted back to the first pillow and changed the subject. "Poor Ruth," he said, "didn't seem to have a very good time."

Joan rose, regal in her high-waisted, floor-length, powder-blue party dress, and seized the brandy bottle on the piano; its long neck became a sceptre in her hand. She took up a dirty snifter, tossed its residue into the fireplace, listened to the sizzle, and poured herself a tawny, chortling slug. "Poor Ruth," she repeated carefully, seating herself again in the director's chair.

"Of course," Richard amplified, "why *should* she have a good time, with that jerk for a husband?"

"Jerry's not such a jerk," Joan said. "He's a lovely dancer, for one thing. A good athlete. There's a lot you could learn from him."

"No doubt." He thought the subject should be changed back again. "If Marlene's just my red herring," he asked, "why did she dance with me so long?"

"Maybe you're hers. We can have red herrings too, you know. Women's lib."

"Then who's Marlene really seeing?"

"Jerry?"

"Impossible."

"Why are you so sure?"

"Because he's such a jerk. All he can do is talk stocks, throw the football, and dance." Every time, that fall, playing touch football, he had caught a pass thrown from Jerry's hand, Richard had felt guilt tag him.

Joan's smile sealed upon a swallow of brandy. "A jerk," she said, "can be a fish."

"There are fish in your game too?"

The brandy produced eloquence. "What are these boring messy parties for except fishing? If you've caught your fish, you go to see him. Or her. If you haven't yet, you go in hopes you will. If you don't fish at all, like the Donnelsons, you go out of fascination, to see who's catching what. And we need them, too. Like fish need water to swim in."

"We? Whose fish are you? You make that brandy look awful good."

Joan rose and brought the bottle to him, because, Richard figured, she could pour herself another splash on the way, and because she knew she looked better standing up in her queenly dress than sitting down. Sitting down, she looked pregnant. "First," she responded, having served him and reseated herself, while the front of her waist puffed up in a nostalgic simulation of childbearing, "let's figure out, whose red herring am I?"

"You *were* Mack's," Richard ventured, "but that seems to have cooled. He was all over Eleanor tonight; do you think they're going to get remarried?"

"And waste all those lawyers' fees?"

"Jerry's," he tried. "You danced with him twice, on and on." Irate, truth seeming to dawn, Richard sat up and pointed accusingly. "You're that jerk's red herring!"

"I am not," Joan replied calmly. "Jerry and I talked a long time, but it was about you and Ruth."

"Oh. And what did you decide?"

"That the two of you weren't doing anything really."

"How nice." His relief blended with annoyance at her complacent underestimation.

"If there *were* something going on," Joan continued, "you'd speak to each other at least *once* at a party, for appearances' sake. As is, you just stare. The question is, are you working up to something? I think so, he doesn't. He's very sure of her."

"He would be. What a jerk."

His tone, too vehement, seemed to offend her, in her queenly blue dress. "Let's talk about *me*," Joan said. "I'm tired of talking about you."

"What *about* you? Are you fishing?"

"Do I act it?"

He thought. "I think," he said, "you're a flirt, but not a fisherwoman."

"You don't think I have the guts?"

"You have the guts," he said, "but not the—the what? The *edge*. Every time you feel an edge working up, you hit yourself with another slug of brandy and dull it. Like now. This could be a pretty sexy talk; but by the time we get upstairs you'll be dead. Hey. It just occurred to me why Jim left. It wasn't my dancing with Marlene at all, nobody gives a damn who their wife dances with. It was *your* dancing so long with Jerry. Jim is your fish, and you teased him with your red herring."

"Don't let my theory run away with you."

"It makes sense. You used to be Mack's fish, and now you're his red herring, while he makes up to Eleanor, or is Eleanor *his* red herring, and—did you notice how much time he spent talking to Linda Donnelson?"

Joan's face froze, for the briefest moment: the way a gust of wind will suddenly flatten choppy water. "Linda? Don't be silly. They were arguing about low-income housing."

Why was she defensive? Had she gone back to Mack? Richard doubted this; their affair had cooled as soon as Mack got divorced. It was the mention of the Donnelsons. "For that matter," he ventured, "you don't seem to think Sam is as boring as you used to."

"He *is* boring. I talked to him because I was the hostess and nobody else would."

"He does have a gorgeous body," Richard admitted, as if she had asserted this. "Once you get below his wooden head."

"Is it so wooden?"

"I don't know, is it? You're the one who's tapping it."

"I'm not tapping anything. I'm sitting here looking at you and thinking I don't like you very much."

"That time Sam took us sailing," Richard went on, "I was struck by what a terrific muscular back he has with his shirt off. Why did he ask us sailing? He knows I have hydrophobia. Whereas you turned out to be a regular little salt, fluttering up there with the jib sheet. How is it, in a boat? Anything like a waterbed? God, sweetie, you have your nerve, bringing up the Donnelsons and telling me what innocent *aqua pura* they were. So Sam's your fish. Landed or not. I still can't figure out who your red herring is, you have so many."

Her silence frightened him; he became again a little boy begging his mother to speak to him, to rescue him from drowning in the blood-deep currents of her moods, of her secrets. "Tell me some more," he begged Joan, "about why you don't like me. It's music to my ears."

"You're cruel," she pronounced, the brandy glass resting in her hand like a symbolic orb of power, "and you're greedy."

"Now tell me why you like me. Tell me why we shouldn't get a divorce."

"I hate your ego," she said, "and our sex is lousy, but I've never been lonely with you. I've never for an instant felt alone when you were in the room." Tears made her blink, and end.

He blinked also, out of weariness. "Well that's a pretty weak endorsement. It won't sell much of the product in Peoria."

"Is that what we're trying to do? Sell the product in Peoria?"

"It sure as hell isn't selling very well here. Except to red herrings and poor fish."

His attack flustered her, routed her from her throne. "You shouldn't get angry," she said, standing, "when I try to talk. It doesn't happen that often." She began to collect glasses, and to carry them toward the kitchen.

"Thank God for that. You're appalling."

"What is it that offends you? That I'm even a little bit alive?"

"Alive for other people, but not for me."

"You sounded just like Ruth, saying that. You've

even caught her self-pity. Come on. Help me clean up this mess."

"A mess it is," he admitted. But clearing it away, arranging all these receptacles in the racks of the dishwasher and then shepherding them back, spotless, to their allotted spaces in the cupboard, felt like another layer of confusion, a cover-up. Richard stayed on the sofa, trying to see through the tangle to the light. Joan was on to Ruth; that space was gone. There remained one area of opportunity, one way to beat the system; its simplicity made him smile. Sleep with your red herring.

Sublimating

The Maples agreed that, since sex was the only sore point in their marriage, they should give it up: sex, not the marriage, which was eighteen years old and stretched back to a horizon where even their birth pangs, with a pang, seemed to merge. A week went by. On Saturday, Richard brought home in a little paper bag a large raw round cabbage. Joan asked, "What is *that?*"

"It's just a cabbage."

"What am I supposed to *do* with it?" Her irritability gratified him.

"You don't have to do *any*thing with it. I saw

Mack Dennis go into the A & P and went in to talk to him about the new environment commission, whether they weren't muscling in on the conservation committee, and then I had to buy something to get out through the check-out counter so I bought this cabbage. It was an impulse. You know what an impulse is." Rubbing it in. "When I was a kid," he went on, "we always used to have a head of cabbage around; you could cut a piece off to nibble instead of a candy. The hearts were best. They really burned your mouth."

"O.K., O.*K*." Joan turned her back and resumed washing dishes. "Well I don't know where you're going to put it; since Judith turned vegetarian the refrigerator's already so full of vegetables I could cry."

Her turning her back aroused him; it usually did. He went closer and thrust the cabbage between her face and the sink. "*Look* at it, darley. Isn't it beautiful? It's so perfect." He was only partly teasing; he had found himself, in the A & P, ravished by the glory of the pyramided cabbages, the mute and glossy beauty that had waited thirty years for him to rediscover it. Not since preadolescence had his senses opened so innocently wide: the pure sphericity, the shy cellar odor, the solid heft. He chose, not the largest cabbage, but the roundest, the most ideal, and carried it naked in his hand to the check-out counter, where the girl, with a flicker of surprise, dressed it in a paper bag and charged him 33¢. As he drove the mile home, the secret sphere beside him in the seat seemed a hole he had drilled back into reality. And now, cutting a slice from one pale cheek, he marveled across the years at the miracle of the wound, at the tender compaction of the leaves, each tuned to its curve as tightly as a guitar string. The taste was blander than his childhood memory of it, but the texture was delicious in his mouth.

Bean, their baby, ten, came into the kitchen. "What is Daddy eating?" she asked, looking into the empty bag for cookies. She knew Daddy as a snack-sneaker.

"Daddy bought himself a cabbage," Joan told her.

The child looked at her father with eyes in which amusement had been pre-prepared; there was a serious warmth that Mommy and animals, especially horses, gave off, and everything else had the coolness of comedy. "That was silly," she said.

"Nothing silly about it," Richard said. "Have a bite." He offered her the cabbage as if it were an apple. Inside her round head he envisioned leaves and leaves of female psychology, packed so snugly the wrinkles dovetailed.

Bean made a spitting face and harshly laughed.

"That's nasty," she said. Bolder, brighter-eyed, flirting. "*You're* nasty." Trying it out.

Hurt, Richard said to her, "I don't like you either. I just like my cabbage." And he kissed the cool pale dense vegetable once, twice, on the cheek; Bean gurgled in astonishment.

Her back still turned, Joan continued from the sink, "If you *had* to buy something, I wish you'd remembered Calgonite. I've been doing the dishes by hand for days."

"Remember it yourself," he said. "Where's the Saran Wrap for my cabbage?" But, as the week wore on, the cabbage withered; the crisp planar wound of each slice by the next day had browned and loosened. Stubbornly loyal, Richard cut and nibbled his slow way to the heart, which burned on his tongue so sharply that his taste buds even in their adult dullness were not disappointed; he remembered how it had been, the oilcloth-covered table where his grandmother used to "schnitz" cabbage into strings for sauerkraut and give him the leftover raw hearts for a snack. He did not buy another cabbage, once the first was eaten; analogously, he never returned to a mistress, once Joan had discovered and mocked her. Their eyes, that is, had married and merged to three, and in the middle shared one her dry female-to-female clarity would always oust his erotic mists.

• • •

Her lovers, on the other hand, he never discovered while she had them. Months or even years later she would present an affair to him complete, self-packaged as nicely as a cabbage, the man remarried and moved to Seattle, her own wounds licked in secrecy and long healed. So he knew, coming home one evening and detecting a roseate afterglow in her face, that he would discover only some new wrinkle of innocence. Nevertheless, he asked, "What have *you* been up to today?"

"Same old grind. After school I drove Judith to her dance lesson, Bean to the riding stable, Dickie to the driving range."

"Where was John?"

"He stayed home with me and said it was boring. I told him to go build something so he's building a guillotine in the cellar; he says the sixth grade is studying revolution this term."

"What's he using for a blade?"

"He flattened an old snow shovel he says he can get sharp enough."

Richard could hear the child banging and whistling below him. "Jesus, he better not lose a finger." His thoughts flicked from the finger to himself to his wife's even white teeth to the fact that two weeks had passed since they gave up sex.

Casually she unfolded her secret. "One fun thing, though."

"You're taking up yoga again."

"Don't be silly; I was never anything to him. No. There's an automatic car wash opened up downtown, behind the pizza place. You put three quarters in and stay in the car and it just happens. It's hilarious."

"*What* happens?"

"Oh, you know. Soap, huge brushes that come whirling around. It really does quite a good job. Afterwards, there's a little hose you can put a dime in to vacuum the inside."

"I think this is very sinister. The people who are always washing their cars are the same people behind our boys in Vietnam. Furthermore, it's bad for it. The dirt protects the paint."

"It needed it. We're living in the mud now."

Last year, they had moved to an old farmhouse surrounded by vegetation that had been allowed to grow wild. This spring, they attacked the tangle of Nature around them with ominously different styles. Joan raked away dead twigs beneath bushes and pruned timidly, as if she were giving her boys a haircut. Richard scorned such pampering and attacked the problem at the root, or near the root. He wrestled vines from the barn roof, shingles popping and flying; he clipped the barberries down to yellow stubble; he began to prune some overweening yews by the front door and was unable to stop until each branch became a stump. The yews, a rare Japanese variety, had pink soft wood maddeningly like flesh. For days thereafter, the stumps bled amber.

The entire family was shocked, especially the two boys, who had improvised a fort in the cavity under the yews. Richard defended himself: "It was them or me. I couldn't get in my own front door."

"They'll never grow again, Dad," Dickie told him. "You didn't leave any green. There can't be any photosynthesis." The boy's own eyes were green; he kept brushing back his hair from them, with that nervous ladylike gesture of his generation.

"Good," Richard stated. He lifted his pruning clippers, which had an elbow hinge for extra strength, and asked, "How about a haircut?"

Dickie's eyes rounded with fright and he backed closer to his brother, who, though younger, had even longer hair. They looked like two chunky girls, blocking the front door. "Or why don't you both go down to the cellar and stick your heads in the guillotine?" Richard suggested. In a few powerful motions he mutilated a flowering trumpet vine. He had a vision, of right angles, clean clapboards, unclouded windows, level and transparent spaces from which the organic—the impudent, importunate, unceasingly swelling organic—had been finally scoured.

"Daddy's upset about something else, not about your hair," Joan explained to Dickie and John at dinner. As the pact wore on, the family gathered more closely about her; even the cats, he noticed, hesitated to take scraps from his hand.

"What about, then?" Judith asked, looking up from her omelette. She was sixteen and Richard's only ally.

Joan answered, "Something grown-up." Her older daughter studied her for a moment, alertly, and Richard held his breath, thinking she might *see.* Female to female. The truth. The translucent vista of scoured space that was in Joan like a crystal tunnel.

But the girl was too young and, sensing an enemy, attacked her reliable old target, Dickie. "*You,*" she said. "I don't ever see *you* trying to help Daddy, all you do is make Mommy drive you to golf courses and ski mountains."

"Yeah? What about *you,*" he responded weakly, beaten before he started, "making Mommy cook two meals all the time because you're too *pure* to sully your lips with *an*imal matter."

"At least when I'm here I try to help; I don't just sit around reading books about dumb Billy Caster."

"Casper," Richard and Dickie said in unison.

Judith rose to her well-filled height; her bell-bottom hip-hugging Levi's dropped an inch lower and exposed a mingled strip of silken underpants and pearly belly. "I think it's a*tro*cious for some people like us to have too many bushes and people in the ghetto don't even have a weed to look at, they have to go up on their rooftops to breathe. It's *true*, Dickie; don't make that face!"

Dickie was squinting in pain; he found his sister's body painful. "The young sociologist," he said, "flaunting her charms."

"You don't even know what a sociologist is," she told him, tossing her head. Waves of fleshly agitation rippled down toward her toes. "You are a very *spoiled* and *self*ish and *lim*ited person."

"Puh puh, big mature," was all he could say, poor little boy overwhelmed by this blind blooming.

Judith had become an optical illusion in which they all saw different things: Dickie saw a threat, Joan saw herself of twenty-five years ago, Bean saw another large warmth-source that, unlike horses, could read her a bedtime story. John, bless him, saw nothing, or, dimly, an old pal receding. Richard couldn't look. In the evening, when Joan was putting the others to bed, Judith would roll around on the sofa while he tried to read in the chair opposite. "Look, Dad. See my stretch exercises." He was reading *My Million-Dollar Shots,* by Billy Casper. The body must be coiled, tension should be felt in the back muscles and along the left leg at top of backswing. Illustrations, with arrows. The body on the sofa was twisting into lithe knots; Judith was double-jointed and her prowess at yoga may have been why Joan stopped doing it, outshone. Richard glanced up and saw his daughter arched like a staple, her hands gripping her ankles; a glossy bulge of supple belly held a navel at its acme. At the top of the backswing, forearm and back of the left hand should form a straight line. He tried it; it felt awkward. He was a born wrist-collapser. Judith watched him pondering his own wrist and giggled; then she kept giggling, insistently, flirting, trying it out. "Daddy's a narcissist." In the edge of his vision she seemed to be tickling herself and flicking her hair in circles.

"Judith!" He had not spoken to her so sharply since, at the age of three, she had spilled sugar all over the kitchen floor. In apology he added, "You are driving me crazy."

The fourth week, he went to New York, on business. When he returned, Joan told him during their kitchen drink, "This afternoon, everybody was being so cranky, you off, the weather lousy, I piled them all into the car, everybody except Judith; she's spending the night at Margaret Leonard's—"

"You *let* her? With that little bitch and her druggy crowd? Are there going to be boys there?"

"I didn't ask. I hope so."

"Live vicariously, huh?"

He wondered if he could punch her in the face and at the same time grab the glass in her hand so it wouldn't break. It was from a honeymoon set of turquoise Mexican glass of which only three were left. With their shared eye she saw his calculations and her face went stony. Break his fist on that face. "Are you going to let me finish my story?"

"Sure. *Dîtes-moi*, Scheherazade."

"The dog was hilarious, she kept barking and chasing the brushes around and around the car trying to defend us. It took her three rotations to figure out that if it went one way it would be coming back the other. Everybody absolutely howled; we had Danny Vetter in the car with us, and one of Bean's horsy friends; it was a real orgy." Her face went rosy, recalling.

"That is a truly disgusting story. Speaking of disgusting, I did something strange in New York."

"You slept with a prostitute."

"Almost. I went to a blue movie."

"How scary for you, darley."

"Well, it was. Wednesday morning I woke up early and didn't have any appointment until eleven so I wandered over to Forty-second Street, you know, with this innocent morning light on everything, and these little narrow places were already open. So—can you stand this?"

"Sure. All I've heard all week are children's complaints."

"I paid three bucks and went in. It was totally dark. Like a fun house at a fairground. Except for this very bright pink couple up on the screen. I could hear people breathing but not see anything. Every time I tried to slide into a row I kept sticking my thumb into somebody's eye. But nobody groaned or protested. It was like those bodies half-frozen in whatever circle it was of Hell. Finally I found a seat and sat down and after a while I could see it was all men, asleep. At least most of them seemed to be asleep. And they were spaced so no two touched; but even at this hour, the place was half full. Of motionless men." He felt her disappointment; he hadn't conveyed the fairytale magic of the experience: the darkness absolute as lead, the undercurrent of snoring as from a single dragon, the tidy way the men had spaced themselves, like checkers on a board. And then how he had found a blank square, had jumped himself, as it were, into it, had joined humanity in stunned witness of its own process of perpetuation.

Joan asked, "How was the movie?"

"Awful. Exasperating. You begin to think entirely in technical terms: camera position, mike boom. And the poor cunts, God, how they work. Apparently to get a job in a blue movie a man has to be A, blond, and B, impotent."

"Yes," Joan said and turned her back, as if to conceal a train of thought. "We have to go to dinner tonight with the new Dennises." Mack Dennis had remarried, a woman much like Eleanor only slightly younger and, the Maples agreed, not nearly as nice. "They'll keep us up forever. But maybe tomorrow," Joan was going on, as if to herself, timidly, "after the kids go their separate ways, if you'd like to hang around . . . "

"No," he took pleasure in saying. "I'm determined to play golf. Thursday afternoon one of the accounts took me out to Long Island and even with borrowed clubs I was hitting the drives a mile. I think I'm on to something; it's all up here." He showed her the top of his backswing, the stiff left wrist. "I must have been getting twenty extra yards." He swung his empty arms down and through.

"See," Joan said, gamely accepting his triumph as her own, "you're sublimating."

• • •

In the car to the Dennises', he asked her, "How is it?"

"It's quite wonderful, in a way. It's as if my senses are jammed permanently open. I feel all one with Nature. The jonquils are out behind the shed and I just looked at them and cried. They were so beautiful I couldn't stand it. I can't keep myself indoors, all I want to do is rake and prune and push little heaps of stones around."

"You know," he told her sternly, "the lawn isn't just some kind of carpet to keep sweeping, you have to make some decisions. Those lilacs, for instance, are full of dead wood."

"Don't," Joan whimpered, and cried, as darkness streamed by, torn by headlights.

In bed after the Dennises' (it was nearly two; they were numb on brandy; Mack had monologued about conservation and Mrs. Dennis about interior decoration, of "her" house, that the Maples still thought of as Eleanor's), Joan confessed to Richard, "I keep having this little vision—it comes to me anywhere, in the middle of sunshine—of me dead."

"Dead of what?"

"I don't know that, all I know is that I'm dead and it doesn't much matter."

"Not even to the children?"

"For a day or two. But everybody manages."

"Sweetie." He repressed his strong impulse to turn and touch her. He explained, "It's part of being one with Nature."

"I suppose."

"I have it very differently. I keep having this funeral fantasy. How full the church will be, what Spence will say about me in his sermon, who'll be there." Specifically, whether the women he has loved will come and weep with Joan. In his image of this, their combined grief at his eternal denial of himself to them, he glimpsed a satisfaction for which the transient satisfactions of the living flesh were a flawed and feeble prelude; love is merely the backswing. In death, he felt, as he floated on his back in bed, he would grow to his true size.

Joan with their third eye may have sensed his thoughts; where usually she would roll over and turn her back, whether as provocation or withdrawal it was up to him to decide, now she lay paralyzed, parallel to him. "I suppose," she offered, "in a way, it's cleansing. I mean you think of all that energy that went into the Crusades."

"Yes, I think," Richard agreed, unconvinced, "we may be on to something."

Nakedness

"Oh, look," Joan Maple said, in her voice of delight. "We're being invaded!"

Richard Maple lifted his head from the sand.

Another couple, younger, was walking down the beach like a pair of creatures, tawny, maned, their movements made stately by their invisible effort to control self-consciousness. One had to look hard to see that they were naked. A summer's frequentation of the nudist section up the beach, around the point from the bourgeois, bathing-suited section where the Maples lay with their children and their books and their towels and tubes of lotion, had bestowed upon the bodies of this other couple the smooth pelt of an even tan. The sexual signs so large in our interior mythology, the breasts and pubic patches, melted to almost nothing in the middle distance, in the sun. Even the young man's penis seemed incidental. And the young woman appeared a lesser version of the male—the same taut, magnetic stride, the same disturbingly generic arrangement of limbs, abdomen, torso, and skull.

Richard suppressed a grunt. Silence attended the two nudes, pushing out from their advance like wavelets up the packed sand into the costumed people, away from the unnoticing commotion and self-absorbed sparkle of the sea.

"Well!": a woman's exclamation, from underneath an umbrella, blew down the beach like a sandwich wrapper. One old man, his dwindled legs linked to a barrel chest by boyish trunks of plaid nylon, stood up militantly, helplessly, drowning in this assault, making an uplifted gesture between that of hailing a taxi and shaking a fist. Richard's own feelings, he noticed, were hysterically turbulent: a certain political admiration grappled with an immediate sense of social threat; pleasure in the sight of the female was swept under by hatred for the male, whose ally she was publicly declaring herself to be; pleasure in the sight of the male fought specific focus on that superadded, boneless

bit of him, that monkeyish footnote to the godlike thorax; and envy of their youth and boldness and beauty lost itself in an awareness of his own body that washed over him so vividly he involuntarily glanced about for concealment.

His wife, brown and pleased and liberal, said, "They must be stoned."

Abruptly, having paraded several hundred yards, the naked couple turned and ran. The girl, especially, became ridiculous, her buttocks outthrust in the ungainly effort of retreat, her flesh jouncing heavily as she raced to keep up with her mate. He was putting space between them; his hair lifted in a slow spume against the sea's electric blue.

Heads turned as at a tennis match; the spectators saw what had made them run—a policeman walking crabwise off the end of the boardwalk. His uniform made him, too, representative of a species. But as he passed, his black shoes treading the sand in measured pursuit, he was seen as also young, his mustache golden beneath the sad-shaped mirrors of his sunglasses, his arms swinging athletic and brown from his short blue sleeves. Beneath his uniform, for all they knew, his skin wore another uninterrupted tan.

"My God," Richard said softly. "He's one of *them.*"

"He is a pretty young pig," Joan stated with complacent quickness.

Her finding a phrase she so much liked irritated Richard, who had been groping for some paradox, some wordless sadness. The Maples found themselves much together this vacation. One daughter was living with a man, one son had a job, the other son was at a tennis camp, and their baby, Bean, hated her nickname and, at thirteen, was made so uncomfortable by her parents she contrived daily excuses to avoid being with them. In their reduced family they were too exposed to one another; the child saw them, Richard feared, more clearly than he and Joan saw themselves. He suggested, as in college when they were courting he might have suggested they leave the library and go to a movie, "Let's follow him."

The policeman was a receding blue dot. "Let's," Joan agreed, standing promptly, sand raining from her, the gay alacrity of her acceptance hollow but the lustrous volume of her body, and her gait beside his, which he unthinkingly matched, and the weight of warm sun on his shoulders as they walked, real enough—real enough, Richard thought, for now.

The bathing-suited section thinned behind them. As they turned the point, they saw naked bodies. Freckled redheads with slack and milky bellies.

Gypsyish girls hard as nuts, standing upright to hold their faces closer to the sun. Sleeping men, their testicles rotten as dropped fruit. A row of buttocks like the scallop on a doily. A bearded man doing yoga on his head, the fork of his legs appearing to implore the sky. Among these apparitions the policeman moved gently, cumbersome in his belt and gun, whispering, nearly touching the naked listeners, who nodded and began, singly and in groups, to put on their clothes. The couple who had trespassed, inviting this counter-invasion, could not be distinguished from the numerous naked others; all were being punished.

Joan went to a trio, two boys and a girl, as they struggled into their worn jeans, their widths of leather and sleeveless vests, their sandals and strange soft hats. She asked them, "Are you being kicked off?"

The boys straightened and gazed at her—her bikini, her pleasant plumpness, her sympathetic smile—and said nothing. The penis of one boy, Richard noticed, hung heavy a foot from her hand. Joan turned and returned to her husband's side.

"What did they tell you?" he asked.

"Nothing. They just stared at me. Like I was a nincompoop."

"There have been two revolutions in the last ten years," he told her. "One, women learned to say 'fuck.' Two, the oppressed learned to despise their sympathizers."

To soften his words he added, "Or maybe they just resented being approached when they were putting on their pants. It's a touchy moment, for males."

The nudists, paradoxically, brought more clothing to the beach than the bourgeoisie; they distinguished themselves, walking up the beach to the point, by being dressed head to toe, in denim and felt, as if they had strolled straight from the urban core of the counterculture. Now, as the young cop moved among them like a sorrowing angel, they bent and huddled in the obsequious poses of redressing.

"My God," Joan said, "it's like Masaccio's *Expulsion from the Garden.*" And Richard felt her heart in the fatty casing of her body plump up, pleased with this link, satisfied to have demonstrated once again to herself the relevance of a humanistic education to modern experience.

All that afternoon, as, returned from the beach, he pushed a balky lawn mower through the wiry grass around their rented house, Richard thought about nakedness. He thought of Adam and Eve ("Who told thee that thou wast naked?") and of Noah beheld naked by Ham, and of Susanna and the elders. He thought of himself as a child, having a sunbath on the second-story porch with his mother, who had been, in her provincial way, an avant-gardist, a health faddist. Wasps would come visit, the porch was so warm. An hour seemed forever; his embarrassment penetrated and stretched every minute. His mother's skin was a pale landscape on the rim of his vision; he didn't look at it, any more than he bothered to look at the hills enclosing their little West Virginia town, which he assumed he would never leave.

He recalled a remark of Rodin's, that a woman undressing was like the sun piercing through clouds. The afternoon's gathering cloudiness slid shadows across the lawn, burnishing the wiry grass. He had once loved a woman who had slept beside a mirror. In her bed the first time, he glanced to his right and was startled to see them both, reflected naked. His legs and hers looked prodigiously long, parallel. She must have felt his attention leave her, for she turned her head; duplicated in the mirror, her face appeared beneath the duplicate of his. The mirror was an arm's length from the bed. What fascinated him in it was not her body but his own—its length, its glow, its hair, its parallel toes so marvelously removed from its small, startled, sheepish head.

There had been, he remembered, a noise downstairs. Their eyes had widened into one another's, the mirror forgotten. He whispered, "What is it?" Milkmen, mailmen, the dog, the furnace.

She offered, "The wind?"

"It sounded like a door opening."

As they listened again, her breath fanned his mouth. A footstep distinctly betrayed itself beneath them. At the same moment as he tugged to pull the sheets over their heads, she sharply flung them aside. She disengaged herself from him, lifting her leg like the near figure in Renoir's *Bathers*. He was alone in the mirror; the mirror had become a screaming witness to the fact that he was where he should not be ("Dirt is matter in the wrong place," his mother used to say) and that he was in no condition for flight. He had gone onto her sunporch with his bunched clothes clutched to his front.

He squatted now to cut the stubborn tufts by the boat shed with the hand clippers, and imperfectly remembered a quotation from one of the Japanese masters of *shungā*, to the effect that the phallus in these pictures was exaggerated because if it were drawn in its natural size, it would be negligible.

She had returned, his mistress, still naked, saying, "Nothing." She had walked naked through her own downstairs, a trespasser from Eden, past chairs and prints and lamps, eclipsing them, unafraid to encounter a burglar, a milkman, a husband; and her nakedness, returning, had been calm and broad as that of Titian's Venus, flooding him from within like some swallowed sun.

He thought of Titian's Venus, wringing her hair with two firm hands. He thought of Manet's Olympia, of Goya's Maja. Of shamelessness. He thought of Edna Pontellier, Kate Chopin's heroine, walking in the last year of that most buttoned-up of centuries down to the Gulf and, before swimming to her death, casting off all her clothes. "How strange and awful it seemed to stand naked under the sky! How delicious!"

He remembered himself a month ago, coming along to this same house, this house into whose lightless, damp cellar he was easing, step by step, the balky mower, its duty done. He had volunteered to come alone and open up the house, to test it; it was a new rental for them. Joan had assented easily; there was something in her, these days, that also wanted to be alone. Half the stores on the island were not yet open for the summer; he had bought some days' worth of meals, and lived in rooms of a profound chastity and silence. One morning he had walked through a mile of huckleberry and wild grape to a pond. Its rim of beach was scarcely a stride wide; only the turds and shed feathers of wild swans testified to other presences. The swans, suspended in the sun-irradiated mist upon the pond's surface, seemed gods to him, perfect and infinitely removed. Not a house, not a car, looked down from the hills of sand and scrub that enclosed the pond. Such pure emptiness under the sky seemed an opportunity it would be sacrilegious to waste. Richard took off his clothes, all; he sat on a rough warm rock. The pose of thinker palled. He stood and at the water's edge became a prophet, a Baptist; ripples of light reflected from the water onto his legs. He yearned to do something transcendent, something obscene; he stretched his arms and could not touch the sky. The sun intensified. As mist burned from the surface of the pond, the swans stirred, flapping their wings in aloof, Olympian tumult. For a second, sex dropped from him and he seemed indeed the divinely shaped center of a bowl-shaped Creation; his very skin felt beautiful—no, he felt beauty rippling upon it, as if this emptiness were loving him, licking him. Then, the next second, glancing down, he saw himself to be less than sublimely alone, for dozens of busy ruddy bodies, ticks, were crawling up through the hair of his legs, as happy in his giant warmth as he was in the warmth of the sun.

The sky was even gray now, weathered silver like the shingles on this island. As he went into the house to reward himself with a drink, he remembered, from an old sociology text, a nineteenth-century American farmer's boasting that though he had sired eleven children he had never seen his wife's body naked. And from another book, perhaps by John Gunther, the assertion, of some port in West Africa, that this was the last city on the coast where a young woman could walk naked down the main street without attracting attention. And from an old *Time* review, years ago, revolutions ago, of the Brigitte Bardot picture that for a few frames displayed her naked from head to toe: *Time* had quipped that though the movie had a naked woman in it, so did most American homes, around eleven o'clock at night.

Eleven o'clock. The Maples have been out to dinner; their lone child is spending the night with a friend. Their bedroom within this house is white and breezy, white even to the bureaus and chairs, and the ceiling so low their shadows seem to rest upon their heads.

Joan stands at the foot of the bed and kicks off her shoes. Her face, foreshortened in the act of looking down, appears to pout as she undoes the snaps on her skirt and lets the zipper fling into view a white V of slip. She lets her skirt drop, retrieves it with a foot, places it in a drawer. Then the jersey lifts, decapitating her and gathering her hair into a cloud, a fist, that collapses when her face is again revealed, preoccupied. A head-toss, profiled. Auto lights from the road caress the house and then forget. An unexpected sequence: Joan pulls down her underpants in a quick shimmy before—with two hands, arms crossed—pulling up her slip. Above her waist, the bunched nylon snags; she halts in the pose of Michelangelo's slave, of Munch's madonna, of Ingres' urn-bearer, seen from the front, unbarbered. The slip unsnags, the snakeskin slides, the process continues. With a squint of effort she uncouples the snaps at her back and flips the bra toward the hamper in the hall. Her breasts bounce. Toward the bed she says, in her voice of displeasure, "Don't you have something better to do? Than watch me?"

Richard has been lying on the bed half-dressed, an audience of one, holding his applause. He answers truthfully, "No."

He jumps up and finishes undressing, his shadow whirling about his head. The two of them stand close, as close as at the beach when she had returned from being rejected by the young men and he had taunted her. They are back on the beach; she is remembering. Again he feels her heart in the fatty casing of her body plump up, pleased. She looks at him, her eyes blue as a morning sea, and smiles. "*No,*" Joan says, in complacent denial. Richard feels thrilled, invaded. This nakedness is new to them.

Separating

The day was fair. Brilliant. All that June the weather had mocked the Maples' internal misery with solid sunlight—golden shafts and cascades of green in which their conversations had wormed unseeing, their sad murmuring selves the only stain in Nature. Usually by this time of the year they had acquired tans; but when they met their elder daughter's plane on her return from a year in England they were almost as pale as she, though Judith was too dazzled by the sunny opulent jumble of her native land to notice. They did not spoil her homecoming by telling her immediately. Wait a few days, let her recover from jet lag, had been one of their formulations, in that string of gray dialogues —over coffee, over cocktails, over Cointreau—that had shaped the strategy of their dissolution, while the earth performed its annual stunt of renewal unnoticed beyond their closed windows. Richard had thought to leave at Easter; Joan had insisted they wait until the four children were at last assembled, with all exams passed and ceremonies attended, and the bauble of summer to console them. So he had drudged away, in love, in dread, repairing screens, getting the mowers sharpened, rolling and patching their new tennis court.

The court, clay, had come through its first winter pitted and windswept bare of redcoat. Years ago the Maples had observed how often, among their friends, divorce followed a dramatic home improvement, as if the marriage were making one last strong effort to live; their own worst crisis had come amid the plaster dust and exposed plumbing of a kitchen renovation. Yet, a summer ago, as canary-yellow bulldozers gaily churned a grassy, daisy-dotted knoll into a muddy plateau, and a crew of pigtailed young men raked and tamped clay into a plane, this transformation did not strike them as ominous, but festive in its impudence; their marriage could rend the earth for fun. The next spring, waking each day at dawn to a sliding sensation as if the bed were being tipped, Richard found the barren tennis court—its net and tapes still rolled in the barn—an environment congruous with his mood of purposeful desolation, and the crumbling of handfuls of clay into cracks and holes (dogs had frolicked on the court in a thaw; rivulets had evolved trenches) an activity suitably elemental and interminable. In his sealed heart he hoped the day would never come.

Now it was here. A Friday. Judith was reacclimated; all four children were assembled, before jobs and camps and visits again scattered them. Joan thought they should be told one by one. Richard was for making an announcement at the table. She said, "I think just making an announcement is a cop-out. They'll start quarreling and playing to each other instead of focusing. They're each individuals, you know, not just some corporate obstacle to your freedom."

"O.K., O.K. I agree." Joan's plan was exact. That evening, they were giving Judith a belated welcome-home dinner, of lobster and champagne. Then, the party over, they, the two of them, who nineteen years before would push her in a baby carriage along Fifth Avenue to Washington Square, were to walk her out of the house, to the bridge across the salt creek, and tell her, swearing her to secrecy. Then Richard Jr., who was going directly from work to a rock concert in Boston, would be told, either late when he returned on the train or early Saturday morning before he went off to his job; he was seventeen and employed as one of a golf-course maintenance crew. Then the two younger children, John and Margaret, could, as the morning wore on, be informed.

"Mopped up, as it were," Richard said.

"Do you have any better plan? That leaves you the rest of Saturday to answer any questions, pack, and make your wonderful departure."

"No," he said, meaning he had no better plan, and agreed to hers, though to him it showed an edge of false order, a hidden plea for control, like Joan's long chore lists and financial accountings and, in the days when he first knew her, her too-copious lecture notes. Her plan turned one hurdle for him into four—four knife-sharp walls, each with a sheer blind drop on the other side.

All spring he had moved through a world of insides and outsides, of barriers and partitions. He and Joan stood as a thin barrier between the children and the truth. Each moment was a partition, with the past on one side and the future on the other, a future containing this unthinkable *now*. Beyond four knifelike walls a new life for him waited vaguely. His skull cupped a secret, a white face, a face both frightened and soothing, both strange and known, that he wanted to shield from tears, which he felt all about him, solid as the sunlight. So haunted, he had become obsessed with battening down the house against his absence, replacing screens and sash cords, hinges and latches —a Houdini making things snug before his escape.

The lock. He had still to replace a lock on one of the doors of the screened porch. The task, like most such, proved more difficult than he had imagined. The old lock, aluminum frozen by corrosion, had been deliberately rendered obsolete by manufacturers. Three hardware stores had nothing that even approximately matched the mortised hole its removal (surprisingly easy) left. Another hole had to be gouged, with bits too small and saws too big, and the old hole fitted with a block of wood— the chisels dull, the saw rusty, his fingers thick with lack of sleep. The sun poured down, beyond the porch, on a world of neglect. The bushes already needed pruning, the windward side of the house was shedding flakes of paint, rain would get in when he was gone, insects, rot, death. His family, all those he would lose, filtered through the edges of his awareness as he struggled with screw holes, splinters, opaque instructions, minutiae of metal.

Judith sat on the porch, a princess returned from exile. She regaled them with stories of fuel shortages, of bomb scares in the Underground, of Pakistani workmen loudly lusting after her as she walked past on her way to dance school. Joan came and went, in and out of the house, calmer than she should have been, praising his struggles with the lock as if this were one more and not the last of their long chain of shared chores. The younger of his sons, John, now at fifteen suddenly, unwittingly handsome, for a few minutes held the rickety screen door while his father clumsily hammered and chiseled, each blow a kind of sob in Richard's ears. His younger daughter, having been at a slumber party, slept on the porch hammock through all the noise—heavy and pink, trusting and forsaken. Time, like the sunlight, continued relentlessly; the sunlight slowly slanted. Today was one of the longest days. The lock clicked, worked. He was through. He had a drink; he drank it on the porch, listening to his daughter. "It was so sweet," she was saying, "during the worst of it, how all the butchers and bakery shops kept open by candlelight. They're all so plucky and cute. From the papers, things sounded so much worse here—people shooting people in gas lines, and everybody freezing."

Richard asked her, "Do you still want to live in England forever?" *Forever:* the concept, now a reality upon him, pressed and scratched at the back of his throat.

"No," Judith confessed, turning her oval face to him, its eyes still childishly far apart, but the lips set as over something succulent and satisfactory. "I was anxious to come home. I'm an American." She was a woman. They had raised her; he and Joan had endured together to raise her, alone of the four. The others had still some raising left in them. Yet it was the thought of telling Judith—the image of her, their first baby, walking between them arm in arm to the bridge—that broke him. The partition between his face and the tears broke. Richard sat down to the celebratory meal with the back of his throat aching; the champagne, the lobster seemed phases of sunshine; he saw them and tasted them through tears. He blinked, swallowed, croakily joked about hay fever. The tears would not stop leaking through; they came not through a hole that could be plugged but through a permeable spot in a membrane, steadily, purely, endlessly, fruitfully. They became, his tears, a shield for himself against these others—their faces, the fact of their assembly, a last time as innocents, at a table where he sat the last time as head. Tears dropped from his nose as he broke the lobster's back; salt flavored his champagne as he sipped it; the raw clench at the back of his throat was delicious. He could not help himself.

His children tried to ignore his tears. Judith, on his right, lit a cigarette, gazed upward in the direction of her too energetic, too sophisticated exhalation; on her other side, John earnestly bent his face to the extraction of the last morsels—legs, tail segments—from the scarlet corpse. Joan, at the opposite end of the table, glanced at him surprised, her reproach displaced by a quick grimace, of forgiveness, or of salute to his superior gift of strategy. Between them, Margaret, no longer called Bean, thirteen and large for her age, gazed from the other side of his pane of tears as if into a shopwindow at something she coveted—at her father, a crystalline heap of splinters and memories. It was not she, however, but John who, in the kitchen, as they cleared the plates and carapaces away, asked Joan the question: *"Why is Daddy crying?"*

Richard heard the question but not the murmured answer. Then he heard Bean cry, "Oh, no-oh!"—the faintly dramatized exclamation of one who had long expected it.

John returned to the table carrying a bowl of salad. He nodded tersely at his father and his lips shaped the conspiratorial words "She told."

"Told what?" Richard asked aloud, insanely.

The boy sat down as if to rebuke his father's distraction with the example of his own good manners. He said quietly, "The separation."

Joan and Margaret returned; the child, in Richard's twisted vision, seemed diminished in size, and relieved, relieved to have had the bogieman at last proved real. He called out to her—the distances at the table had grown immense—"You knew, you always knew," but the clenching at the back of his throat prevented him from making sense of it. From afar he heard Joan talking, levelly, sensibly, reciting what they had prepared: it was a separation for the summer, an experiment. She and Daddy both agreed it would be good for them; they needed space and time to think; they liked each other but did not make each other happy enough, somehow.

Judith, imitating her mother's factual tone, but in her youth off-key, too cool, said, "I think it's silly. You should either live together or get divorced."

Richard's crying, like a wave that has crested and crashed, had become tumultuous; but it was overtopped by another tumult, for John, who had been so reserved, now grew larger and larger at the table. Perhaps his younger sister's being credited with knowing set him off. "Why didn't you *tell* us?" he asked, in a large round voice quite unlike his own. "You should have *told* us you weren't getting along."

Richard was startled into attempting to force words through his tears. "We *do* get along, that's the trouble, so it doesn't show even to us—" *That we do not love each other* was the rest of the sentence; he couldn't finish it.

Joan finished for him, in her style. "And we've always, *especially*, loved our children."

John was not mollified. "What do you care about *us?*" he boomed. "We're just little things you *had.*" His sisters' laughing forced a laugh from him, which he turned hard and parodistic: "Ha ha *ha.*" Richard and Joan realized simultaneously that the child was drunk, on Judith's homecoming champagne. Feeling bound to keep the center of the stage, John took a cigarette from Judith's pack, poked it into his mouth, let it hang from his lower lip, and squinted like a gangster.

"You're not little things we had," Richard called to him. "You're the whole point. But you're grown. Or almost."

The boy was lighting matches. Instead of holding them to his cigarette (for they had never seen him smoke; being "good" had been his way of setting himself apart), he held them to his mother's face, closer and closer, for her to blow out. Then he lit the whole folder—a hiss and then a torch, held against his mother's face. Prismed by his tears, the flame filled Richard's vision; he didn't know how it was extinguished. He heard Margaret say,

"Oh stop showing off," and saw John, in response, break the cigarette in two and put the halves entirely into his mouth and chew, sticking out his tongue to display the shreds to his sister.

Joan talked to him, reasoning—a fountain of reason, unintelligible. "Talked about it for years . . . our children must help us . . . Daddy and I both want . . ." As the boy listened, he carefully wadded a paper napkin into the leaves of his salad, fashioned a ball of paper and lettuce, and popped it into his mouth, looking around the table for the expected laughter. None came. Judith said, "Be mature," and dismissed a plume of smoke.

Richard got up from this stifling table and led the boy outside. Though the house was in twilight, the outdoors still brimmed with light, the lovely waste light of high summer. Both laughing, he supervised John's spitting out the lettuce and paper and tobacco into the pachysandra. He took him by the hand—a square gritty hand, but for its softness a man's. Yet, it held on. They ran together up into the field, past the tennis court. The raw banking left by the bulldozers was dotted with daisies. Past the court and a flat stretch where they used to play family baseball stood a soft green rise glorious in the sun, each weed and species of grass distinct as illumination on parchment. "I'm sorry, so sorry,"

Richard cried. "You were the only one who ever tried to help me with all the goddam jobs around this place."

Sobbing, safe within his tears and the champagne, John explained, "It's not just the separation, it's the whole crummy year, I *hate* that school, you can't make any friends, the history teacher's a scud."

They sat on the crest of the rise, shaking and warm from their tears but easier in their voices, and Richard tried to focus on the child's sad year—the weekdays long with homework, the weekends spent in his room with model airplanes, while his parents murmured down below, nursing their separation. How selfish, how blind, Richard thought; his eyes felt scoured. He told his son, "We'll think about getting you transferred. Life's too short to be miserable."

They had said what they could, but did not want the moment to heal, and talked on, about the school, about the tennis court, whether it would ever again be as good as it had been that first summer. They walked to inspect it and pressed a few more tapes more firmly down. A little stiltedly, perhaps trying now to make too much of the moment, Richard led the boy to the spot in the field where the view was best, of the metallic blue river, the emerald marsh, the scattered islands velvety with shadow in the low light, the white bits of beach far away. "See," he said. "It goes on being beautiful. It'll be here tomorrow."

"I know," John answered, impatiently. The moment had closed.

Back in the house, the others had opened some white wine, the champagne being drunk, and still sat at the table, the three females, gossiping. Where Joan sat had become the head. She turned, showing him a tearless face, and asked, "All right?"

"We're fine," he said, resenting it, though relieved, that the party went on without him.

In bed she explained, "I couldn't cry I guess because I cried so much all spring. It really wasn't fair. It's your idea, and you made it look as though I was kicking you out."

"I'm sorry," he said. "I couldn't stop. I wanted to but couldn't."

"You *didn't* want to. You loved it. You were having your way, making a general announcement."

"I love having it over," he admitted. "God, those kids were great. So brave and funny." John, returned to the house, had settled to a model airplane in his room, and kept shouting down to them, "I'm O.K. No sweat." "And the way," Richard went on, cozy in his relief, "they never questioned the reasons we gave. No thought of a third person. Not even Judith."

"That *was* touching," Joan said.

He gave her a hug. "You were great too. Very reassuring to everybody. Thank you." Guiltily, he realized he did not feel separated.

"You still have Dickie to do," she told him. These words set before him a black mountain in the darkness; its cold breath, its near weight affected his chest. Of the four children, his elder son was most like a conscience. Joan did not need to add, "That's one piece of your dirty work I won't do for you."

"I know. I'll do it. You go to sleep."

Within minutes, her breathing slowed, became oblivious and deep. It was quarter to midnight. Dickie's train from the concert would come in at one-fourteen. Richard set the alarm for one. He had slept atrociously for weeks. But whenever he closed his lids some glimpse of the last hours scorched them—Judith exhaling toward the ceiling in a kind of aversion, Bean's mute staring, the sun-struck growth of the field where he and John had rested. The mountain before him moved closer, moved within him; he was huge, momentous. The ache at the back of his throat felt stale. His wife slept as if slain beside him. When, exasperated by his hot lids, his crowded heart, he rose from bed and dressed, she awoke enough to turn over. He told her then, "Joan, if I could undo it all, I would."

"Where would you begin?" she asked. There was no place. Giving him courage, she was always giving him courage. He put on shoes without socks in the dark. The children were breathing in their rooms, the downstairs was hollow. In their confusion they had left lights burning. He turned off all but one, the kitchen overhead. The car started. He had hoped it wouldn't. He met only moonlight on the road; it seemed a diaphanous companion, flickering in the leaves along the roadside, haunting his rearview mirror like a pursuer, melting under his headlights. The center of town, not quite deserted, was eerie at this hour. A young cop in uniform kept company with a gang of T-shirted kids on the steps of the bank. Across from the railroad station, several bars kept open. Customers, mostly young, passed in and out of the warm night, savoring summer's novelty. Voices shouted from cars as they passed; an immense conversation seemed in progress. Richard parked and in his weariness put his head on the passenger seat, out of the commotion and wheeling lights. It was as when, in the movies, an assassin grimly carries his mission through the jostle of a carnival—except the movies cannot show the precipitous, palpable slope you cling to within. You cannot climb back down; you can only fall. The synthetic fabric of the car seat, warmed by his cheek, confided to him an ancient, distant scent of vanilla.

A train whistle caused him to lift his head. It was on time; he had hoped it would be late. The slender drawgates descended. The bell of approach tingled happily. The great metal body, horizontally fluted, rocked to a stop, and sleepy teen-agers disembarked, his son among them. Dickie did not show surprise that his father was meeting him at this terrible hour. He sauntered to the car with two friends, both taller than he. He said "Hi" to his father and took the passenger's seat with an exhausted promptness that expressed gratitude. The friends got into the back, and Richard was grateful; a few more minutes' postponement would be won by driving them home.

He asked, "How was the concert?"

"Groovy," one boy said from the back seat.

"It bit," the other said.

"It was O.K.," Dickie said, moderate by nature, so reasonable that in his childhood the unreason of the world had given him headaches, stomach aches, nausea. When the second friend had been dropped off at his dark house, the boy blurted, "Dad, my eyes are killing me with hay fever! I'm out there cutting that mothering grass all day!"

"Do we still have those drops?"

"They didn't do any good last summer."

"They might this." Richard swung a U-turn on

the empty street. The drive home took a few minutes. The mountain was here, in his throat. "Richard," he said, and felt the boy, slumped and rubbing his eyes, go tense at his tone, "I didn't come to meet you just to make your life easier. I came because your mother and I have some news for you, and you're a hard man to get ahold of these days. It's sad news."

"That's O.K." The reassurance came out soft, but quick, as if released from the tip of a spring.

Richard had feared that his tears would return and choke him, but the boy's manliness set an example, and his voice issued forth steady and dry. "It's sad news, but it needn't be tragic news, at least for you. It should have no practical effect on your life, though it's bound to have an emotional effect. You'll work at your job, and go back to school in September. Your mother and I are really proud of what you're making of your life; we don't want that to change at all."

"Yeah," the boy said lightly, on the intake of his breath, holding himself up. They turned the corner; the church they went to loomed like a gutted fort. The home of the woman Richard hoped to marry stood across the green. Her bedroom light burned.

"Your mother and I," he said, "have decided to separate. For the summer. Nothing legal, no divorce yet. We want to see how it feels. For some years now, we haven't been doing enough for each other, making each other as happy as we should be. Have you sensed that?"

"No," the boy said. It was an honest, unemotional answer: true or false in a quiz.

Glad for the factual basis, Richard pursued, even garrulously, the details. His apartment across town, his utter accessibility, the split vacation arrangements, the advantages to the children, the added mobility and variety of the summer. Dickie listened, absorbing. "Do the others know?"

"Yes."

"How did they take it?"

"The girls pretty calmly. John flipped out; he shouted and ate a cigarette and made a salad out of his napkin and told us how much he hated school."

His brother chuckled. "He did?"

"Yeah. The school issue was more upsetting for him than Mom and me. He seemed to feel better for having exploded."

"He did?" The repetition was the first sign that he was stunned.

"Yes. Dickie, I want to tell you something. This last hour, waiting for your train to get in, has been about the worst of my life. I hate this. *Hate* it. My father would have died before doing it to me." He felt immensely lighter, saying this. He had dumped the mountain on the boy. They were home. Moving swiftly as a shadow, Dickie was out of the car, through the bright kitchen. Richard called after him, "Want a glass of milk or anything?"

"No thanks."

"Want us to call the course tomorrow and say you're too sick to work?"

"No, that's all right." The answer was faint, delivered at the door to his room; Richard listened for the slam that went with a tantrum. The door closed normally, gently. The sound was sickening.

Joan had sunk into that first deep trough of sleep and was slow to awake. Richard had to repeat, "I told him."

"What did he say?"

"Nothing much. Could you go say goodnight to him? Please."

She left their room, without putting on a bathrobe. He sluggishly changed back into his pajamas and walked down the hall. Dickie was already in bed, Joan was sitting beside him, and the boy's bedside clock radio was murmuring music. When she stood, an inexplicable light—the moon?—outlined her body through the nightie. Richard sat on the warm place she had indented on the child's narrow mattress. He asked him, "Do you want the radio on like that?"

"It always is."

"Doesn't it keep you awake? It would me."

"No."

"Are you sleepy?"

"Yeah."

"Good. Sure you want to get up and go to work? You've had a big night."

"I want to."

Away at school this winter he had learned for the first time that you can go short of sleep and live. As an infant he had slept with an immobile, sweating intensity that had alarmed his babysitters. In adolescence he had often been the first of the four children to go to bed. Even now, he would go slack in the middle of a television show, his sprawled legs hairy and brown. "O.K. Good boy. Dickie, listen. I love you so much, I never knew how much until now. No matter how this works out, I'll always be with you. Really."

Richard bent to kiss an averted face but his son, sinewy, turned and with wet cheeks embraced him and gave him a kiss, on the lips, passionate as a woman's. In his father's ear he moaned one word, the crucial, intelligent word: "*Why?*"

Why. It was a whistle of wind in a crack, a knife thrust, a window thrown open on emptiness. The white face was gone, the darkness was featureless. Richard had forgotten why.

Gesturing

She told him with a little gesture he had never seen her use before. Joan had called from the station, having lunched with her lover, Richard guessed. He had been babysitting, and Dickie, who now could drive, had taken his father's convertible. Joan's Volvo was new and for several minutes refused to go into first gear for Richard. By the time he had reached the center of town, she had walked down the main street and up the hill to the green. It was September, leafy and warm, yet with a crystal chill on things, an uncanny clarity. Even from a distance they smiled to see one another.

She opened the door and seated herself, fastening the safety belt to silence its chastening buzz. Her face was rosy from her walk, her city clothes looked like a costume, she carried a small package or two, token of her "shopping." Richard tried to pull a U-turn on the narrow street, and in the long moment of his halting and groping for reverse gear she told him. "Darley," she said, and, oddly, tentatively, soundlessly, tapped the fingers of one hand into the palm of the other, a gesture between a child's clap of glee and an adult's signal for attention, "I've decided to kick you out. I'm going to ask you to leave town."

Abruptly full, his heart thumped; it was what he wanted. "O.K.," he said carefully. "If you think you can manage." He glaced sideways at her face to see if she meant it; he could not believe she did. A red, white, and blue mail truck that had braked to a stop behind them tapped its horn, more reminder than rebuke; the Maples were known in the town. They had lived here most of their married life.

Richard found reverse, backed up, completed the turn, and they headed home, skimming. The car, so new and stiff, in motion felt high and light, as if it too had just been vaporized in her little playful clap. "Things are stagnant," she explained, "stuck; we're not going anywhere."

"I will not give her up," he interposed.

"Don't tell me, you've told me."

"Nor do I see you giving him up."

"I would if you asked. Are you asking?"

"No. Horrors. He's all I've got."

"Well then. Go where you want, I think Boston would be most fun for the kids to visit. And the least boring for you."

"I agree. When do you see this happening?" Her profile, in the side of her vision, felt brittle, about to break if he said a wrong word, too rough a word. He was holding his breath, trying to stay up, high and light, like the car. They went over the bump this side of the bridge; cigarette smoke jarred loose from Joan's face.

"As soon as you can find a place," she said. "Next week. Is that too soon?"

"Probably."

"Is this too sad? Do I seem brutal to you?"

"No, you seem wonderful, very gentle and just, as always. It's right. It's just something I couldn't do myself. How can you possibly live without me in town?"

In the edge of his vision her face turned; he turned to see, and her expression was mischievous, brave, flushed. They must have had wine at lunch. "Easy," Joan said. He knew it was a bluff, a brave gesture; she was begging for reprieve. But he held silent, he refused to argue. This way, he had her pride on his side.

The curves of the road poured by, mailboxes, trees some of which were already scorched by the turn of the year. He asked, "Is this your idea, or his?"

"Mine. It came to me on the train. All Andy said was, I seemed to be feeding you all the time." In the weeks since their summer of separated vacations, Richard had been sleeping in a borrowed seaside shack two miles from their home; he tried to cook there, but each evening, as the nights grew shorter, it seemed easier, and kinder to the children, to eat the dinner Joan had cooked. He was used to her cooking; indeed, his body, every cell, was composed of her cooking. Dinner would lead to a post-dinner drink, while the children (two were off at school, two were still homebound) plodded through their homework or stared at television, and drinking would lead to talking, confidences, harsh words, maudlin tears, and an occasional uxorious collapse upward, into bed. She was right; it was not healthy, nor progressive. The twenty years were by, when it would have been convenient to love one another.

He found the apartment in Boston on the second day of hunting. The real-estate agent had red hair, a round bottom, and a mask of makeup worn as if to conceal her youth. Richard felt happy and scared, going up and down stairs behind her. Wearier of him than he was of her, she fidgeted the key into this lock, bucked the door open with her shoulder, and made her little open-handed gesture of helpless display.

The floor was neither wall-to-wall shag nor splintered wood, but black and white tile, like the floor in a Vermeer; he glanced to the window, saw the skyscraper, and knew this would do. The skyscraper, for years suspended in a famous state of incompletion, was a beautiful disaster, famous because it was a disaster (glass kept falling from it) and disastrous because it was beautiful: the architect had had a vision. He had dreamed of an invisible building, though immense; the glass was meant to reflect the sky and the old low brick skyline of Boston, and to melt into the sky. Instead, the windows of mirroring glass kept falling to the street, and were replaced by ugly opacities of black plywood. Yet enough reflecting surface remained to give an impression, through the wavery old window of this sudden apartment, of huge blueness, a vertical cousin to the horizontal huge blueness of the sea that Richard awoke to each morning, in the now bone-deep morning chill of his unheated shack. He said to the redhead, "Fine," and her charcoal eyebrows lifted. His hands trembled as he signed the lease, having written "Sep" in the space for marital status. From a drugstore he phoned the news, not to his wife, whom it would sadden, but to his mistress, equally far away. "Well," he told her in an accusing voice, "I found one. I signed the lease. Incredible. In the middle of all this fine print there was the one simple sentence, 'There shall be no waterbeds.' "

"You sound so shaky."

"I feel I've given birth to a black hole."

"Don't do it, if you don't want to." From the way Ruth's voice paused and faded he imagined she was reaching for a cigarette, or an ashtray, settling herself to a session of lover-babying.

"I do want to. She wants me to. We all want me to. Even the children are turned on. Or pretend to be."

She ignored the "pretend." "Describe it to me."

All he could remember was the floor, and the view of the blue disaster with reflected clouds drifting across its face. And the redhead. She had told him where to shop for food, where to do his laundry. He would have laundry?

"It sounds nice," was Ruth's remote response, when he had finished saying what he could. Two people, one of them a sweating black mailman, were waiting to use the phone booth. He hated the city already, its crowding, its hunger.

"What sounds nice about it?" he snapped.

"Are you so upset? Don't do it if you don't want to."

"Stop *say*ing that." It was a tedious formality both observed, the pretense that they were free, within each of their marriages, to do as they pleased; guilt avoidance was the game, and Ruth had grown expert at it. Her words often seemed not real words but blank counters, phrases of a proscribed etiquette. Whereas his wife's words always opened in, transparent with meaning.

"What else can I say," Ruth asked, "except that I love you?" And at its far end the phone sharply sighed. He could picture the gesture: she had turned her face away from the mouthpiece and forcefully exhaled, in that way she had, expressive of exasperation even when she felt none, of exhaling and simultaneously stubbing out a cigarette smoked not halfway down its length, so it crumpled under her impatient fingers like an angry sentence thought better of. Her conspicuous unthriftiness pained him. All waste pained him. He wanted abruptly to hang up, but saw that, too, as a wasteful, empty gesture, and hung on.

Alone in his apartment, he discovered himself to be a neat and thrifty housekeeper. When a woman left, he would promptly set about restoring his bachelor order, emptying the ashtrays which, if the visitor had been Ruth, brimmed with long pale bodies prematurely extinguished and, if Joan, with butts so short as to be scarcely more than filters. Neither woman, it somehow pleased him to observe, ever made more than a gesture towards cleaning up—the bed a wreck, the dishes dirty, each of his three ashtrays (one glass, one pottery, and one a tin cookie-jar lid) systematically touched, like the bases in baseball. Emptying them, he would smile, depending, at Ruth's messy morgue, or at Joan's nest of filters, discreet as white pebbles in a bowl of narcissi. When he chastised Ruth for stubbing out cigarettes still so long, she pointed out, of course, with her beautiful unblinking assumption of her own primary worth, how much better it was for *her*, for her lungs, to kill the cigarette early; and of course she was right, better other-destructive than self-destructive. Ruth was love, she was life, that was why he loved her. Yet Joan's compulsive economy, her discreet death wish, was as dearly familiar to him as her tiny repressed handwriting and the tight curls of her pubic hair, so Richard smiled emptying her ashtrays also. His smile was a gesture without an audience. He, who had originated his act among parents and grandparents, siblings and pets, and who had developed it for a public of schoolmates and teachers, and who had carried it to new refinements before an initially rapt audience of his own children, could not in solitude stop performing. He had engendered a companion of sorts, a single grand spectator—the blue skyscraper. He felt it with him all the time.

Blue, it showed greener than the sky. For a time Richard was puzzled, why the clouds reflected in it drifted in the same direction as the clouds behind it. With an effort of spatial imagination he perceived that a mirror does not reverse our motion, though it does transpose our ears, and gives our mouths a tweak, so that the face even of a loved one looks unfamiliar and ugly when seen in a mirror, the way she—queer thought!—always sees it. He saw that a mirror posed in its midst would not affect the motion of an army; and often half a reflected cloud matched the half of another beyond the building's edge, moving as one, pierced by a jet trail as though by Cupid's arrow. The disaster sat light on the city's heart. At night, it showed as a dim row of little lights as if a slender ship were sailing the sky, and during a rain or fog it vanished entirely, while the brick chimney pots and ironstone steeples in Richard's foreground swarthily intensified their substance. Even unseen, it was there; so Richard himself, his soul, was always there. He tried to analyze the logic of window replacement, as revealed in the patterns of gap and glass. He detected no logic, just the slow-motion labor of invisible workers, emptying and filling cells of glass with the brainlessness of bees. If he watched for many minutes, he might see, like the condensation of a dewdrop, a blank space go glassy, and reflective, and greenish-blue. Days passed before he realized that, on the old glass near his nose, the wavery panes of his own window, ghostly previous tenants armed with diamonds had scratched initials, names, dates, and, cut deepest and whitest of all, the touching, comical vow, incised in two trisyllabic lines,

With this ring
I thee wed

What a transparent wealth of previous lives overlay a city's present joy! As he walked the streets his own happiness surprised him. He had expected to be sad, guilty, bored. Instead, his days were snugly filled with his lists, his quests for food and hardware, his encounters with such problematical wife-substitutes as the laundromat, where students pored over Hesse and picked at their chins while their clothes tumbled in eternal circular fall, where young black housewives hummed as they folded white linen. What an unexpected pleasure, walking home in the dark hugging to himself clean clothes hot as fresh bread, past the bow windows of Back Bay glowing like display cases. He felt sober and exhilarated and justified at the hour when in the suburbs, rumpled from the commute, he would be into his hurried second pre-dinner drink. He liked the bringing home of food, the tautological satisfaction of cooking a meal and then eating it all, as the radio fed Bach or Bechet into his ears and a book gazed open-faced from the reading stand he had bought; he liked the odd orderly game of consuming before food spoiled and drinking before milk soured. He liked the way airplanes roamed the brown night sky, a second, thinner city laid upon this one, and the way police sirens sang, scooping up some disaster not his. It could not last, such happiness. It was an interim, a holiday. But an oddly clean and just one, rectilinear, dignified, though marred by gaps of sudden fear and disorientation. Each hour had to be scheduled lest he fall through. He moved like a waterbug, like a skipping stone, upon the glassy tense surface of his new life. He walked everywhere. Once he walked to the base of the blue skyscraper, his companion and witness. It was hideous. Heavily planked and chicken-wired tunnels, guarded by barking policemen, protected pedestrians from falling glass and the owners of the building, already millions in the hole, from more lawsuits. Trestles and trucks jammed the cacophonous area. The lower floors were solid plywood, of a Stygian black; the building, so lovely in air, had tangled mucky roots. Richard avoided walking that way again.

When Ruth visited, they played a game, of washing—scouring, with a Brillo pad—one white square of the Vermeer floor, so eventually it would all appear clean. The black squares they ignored. Naked, scrubbing, Ruth seemed on her knees a plump little steed, long hair swinging, soft breasts swaying in rhythm to her energetic circular strokes. Behind, her pubic hair, uncurly, made a kind of nether mane. So lovably strange, she rarely was allowed to clean more than one square. Time, so careful and regular for him, sped for them, and vanished. There seemed time even to talk only at the end, her hand on the door. She asked, "Isn't that building amazing, with the sunset in it?"

"I love that building. And it loves me."

"No. It's me who loves you."

"Can't you share?"

"No."

She felt possessive about the apartment; when he told her Joan had been there too, and, just for "fun," had slept with him, her husband, Ruth wailed into the telephone. "In *our* bed?"

"In *my* bed," he said, with uncharacteristic firmness.

"In your bed," she conceded, her voice husky as

a sleepy child's. When the conversation finally ended, his mistress sufficiently soothed, he had to go lean his vision against his inanimate, giant friend, dimming to mauve on one side, still cerulean on the other, faintly streaked with reflections of high cirrus. It spoke to him, as the gaze of a dumb beast speaks, of beauty and suffering, of a simplicity that must perish, of time. Evening would soften its shade to slate; night would envelop its sides. Richard's focus shortened, and he read, with irritation, for the hundredth time, that impudent, pious marring, that bit of litany, etched bright by the sun's fading fire.

With this ring
I thee wed

Ruth, months ago, had removed her wedding ring. Coming here to embark with him upon an overnight trip, she wore on that naked finger, as a reluctant concession to imposture, an inherited diamond ring. When she held her hand in the sunlight by the window, a planetary system of rainbows wheeled about the room and signalled, he imagined, to the skyscraper. In the hotel in New York, she confided again her indignation at losing her name in the false assumption of his.

"It's just a convenience," he told her. "A gesture."

"But I *like* who I am now," she protested.

That was, indeed, her central jewel, infrangible and bright: she liked who she was. They had gone separate ways and, returning before him, she had asked at the hotel desk for the room key by number.

The clerk asked her her name. It was a policy. He would not give the key to a number.

"And what did you tell him your name was?" Richard asked, in this pause of her story.

In her pause and dark-blue stare, he saw recreated her hesitation when challenged by the clerk. Also, she had been, before her marriage to Jerry, a second-grade teacher, and Richard saw now the manner—prim, fearful, and commanding—with which she must have confronted those roomfuls of children. "I told him Maple."

Richard had smiled. "That sounds right."

Taking Joan out to dinner felt illicit. She suggested it, for "fun," at the end of one of the children's Sundays. He had been two months in Boston, new habits had replaced old, and it was tempting to leave their children, who were bored and found it easier to be bored by television than by this bossy visitor. "Stop telling me you're bored," he had scolded John, the most docile of his children, and the one he felt guiltiest about. "Fifteen is *supposed* to be a boring age. When I was fifteen, I lay around reading science fiction. You lie around looking at *Kung Fu.* At least I was learning to read."

"It's good," the child protested, his adolescent voice cracking in fear of being distracted from an especially vivid piece of slow-motion *tai chi.* Richard, when living here, had watched the program with him often enough to know that it was, in a sense, good, that the hero's oriental passivity, relieved by spurts of mystical violence, was insinuating into the child a system of ethics, just as Richard had taken ideals of behavior from dime movies and comic books—coolness from Bogart, debonair recklessness from Errol Flynn, duality and deceit from Superman.

He dropped to one knee beside the sofa where John, his upper lip fuzzy and his eyebrows manly dark, stoically gazed into the transcendent flickering; Richard's own voice nearly cracked, asking, "Would it be less boring, if Dad still lived here?"

"No-*oh*": the answer was instantaneous and impatient, as if the question had been anticipated. Did the boy mean it? His eyes did not for an instant glance sideways, perhaps out of fear of betraying himself, perhaps out of genuine boredom with grown-ups and their gestures. On television, satisfyingly, gestures killed. Richard rose from his supplicant position, relieved to hear Joan coming down the stairs. She was dressed to go out, in the timeless black dress with the scalloped neckline, and a collar of Mexican silver. He was wary. He must be wary. They had had it. They must have had it.

Yet the cocktails, and the seafood, and the wine, displaced his wariness; he heard himself saying, to the so familiar and so strange face across the table, "She's lovely, and loves me, you know"—he felt embarrassed, like a son suddenly aware that his mother, though politely attentive, is indifferent to the urgency of an athletic contest being described—"but she does spell everything out, and wants everything spelled out to her. It's like being back in the second grade. And the worst thing is, for all this explaining, for all this glorious fucking, she's still not real to me, the way—you are." His voice did break; he had gone too far.

Joan put her left hand, still bearing their wedding ring, flat on the tablecloth in a sensible, level gesture. "She will be," she promised. "It's a matter of time."

The old pattern was still the one visible to the world. The waitress, who had taught their children in Sunday school, greeted them as if their marriage were unbroken; they ate in this restaurant three or four times a year, and were on schedule. They had known the contractor who had built it, this mock-antique wing, a dozen years ago, and then left town, bankrupt, disgraced, and oddly cheerful. His memory hovered between the beams. Another couple, older than the Maples—the husband had once worked with Richard on a town committee—came up to their booth beaming, jollying, in that obligatory American way. Did they know? It didn't much matter, in this nation of temporary arrangements. The Maples jollied back as one, and tumbled loose only when the older couple moved away. Joan gazed after their backs. "I wonder what they have," she asked, "that we didn't?"

"Maybe they had less," Richard said, "so they didn't expect more."

"That's too easy." She was a shade resistant to his veiled compliments; he was grateful. Please resist.

He asked, "How do you think the kids are doing? John seemed withdrawn."

"That's how he is. Stop picking at him."

"I just don't want him to think he has to be your little husband. That house feels huge now."

"You're telling me."

"I'm sorry." He was; he put his hands palms up on the table.

"Isn't it amazing," Joan said, "how a full bottle of wine isn't enough for two people anymore?"

"Should I order another bottle?" He was dismayed, secretly: the waste.

She saw this, and said, "No. Just give me half of what's in your glass."

"You can have it all." He poured.

She said, "So your fucking is really glorious?"

He was embarrassed by the remark now, and feared it set a distasteful trend. As with Ruth there was an etiquette of adultery, so with Joan some code of separation must be maintained. "It usually is," he told her, "between people who aren't married."

"Is dat right, white man?" A swallow of his wine inside her, Joan began to swell with impending hilarity. She leaned as close as the table would permit. "You must *prom*ise"—a gesture went with "promise," a protesting little splaying of her hands —"never to tell this to anybody, not even Ruth."

"Maybe you shouldn't tell me. In fact, don't." He understood why she had been laconic up to now; she had been wanting to talk about her lover, holding him warm within her like a baby. She was going to betray him. "Please don't," Richard said.

"Don't be such a prig. You're the only person I can talk to, it doesn't mean a thing."

"That's what you said about our going to bed in my apartment."

"Did she mind?"

"Incredibly."

Joan laughed, and Richard was struck, for the thousandth time, by the perfection of her teeth, even and rounded and white, bared by her lips as if in proof of a perfect skull, an immaculate soul. Her glee whirled her to a kind of heaven as she confided stories about herself and Andy—how he and a motel manageress had quarreled over the lack of towels in a room taken for the afternoon, how he fell asleep for exactly seven minutes each time after making love. Richard had known Andy for years, a slender swarthy specialist in corporation law, himself divorced, though professionally engaged in the finicking arrangement of giant mergers. A fussy dresser, a churchman, he brought to many occasions an undue dignity and perhaps had been more attracted to Joan's surface glaze, her smooth New England ice, than the mischievous demons underneath. "My psychiatrist thinks Andy was symbiotic with you, and now that you're gone, I can see him as absurd."

"He's not absurd. He's good, loyal, handsome, prosperous. He tithes. He has a twelve handicap. He loves you."

"He protects you from me, you mean. His buttons!—we have to allow a half-hour afterwards for him to do up all his buttons. If they made four-piece suits, he'd wear them. And he washes—he washes *everything*, every time."

"Stop," Richard begged. "Stop telling me all this."

But she was giddy amid the spinning mirrors of her betrayals, her face so flushed and tremulous the waitress sympathetically giggled, pouring the Maples their coffee. Joan's face was pink as a peony, her eyes a blue pale as ice, almost transparent. He saw through her words to what she was saying—that these lovers, however we love them, are not us, are not sacred as reality is sacred. We are reality. We have made children. We gave each other our young bodies. We promised to grow old together.

Joan described an incident in her house, once theirs, when the plumber unexpectedly arrived. Richard had to laugh with her; that house's plumbing problems were an old joke, an ongoing saga. "The backdoor bell rang, Mr. Kelly stomped right in, you know how the kitchen echoes in the bedroom, we had *had* it." She looked, to see if her meaning was clear. He nodded. Her eyes sparkled. She emphasized, of the knock, "Just at the *very* moment," and, with a gesture akin to the gentle clap in the car a world ago, drew with one fingertip a *v* in the air, as if beginning to write "very." The motion was eager, shy, exquisite, diffident, trusting: he saw all its meanings and knew that she would never stop gesturing within him, never; though a decree come between them, even death, her gestures would endure, cut into glass.

Divorcing:
A Fragment

Richard Maple wondered, Can even dying be worse than this? His wife sat crouched on what had been their bed, telling him, between sobs, of her state of mind, which was suicidal, depressive, beaten. They had been living apart for a year and a half, and the time had achieved nothing, no scar tissue had formed, her body was a great unhealed wound crying, *Come back.*

She was growing older; the skin of her face, as she bowed her head to cry, puckered and dripped in little dry points below her eyes, at the corners of her mouth. He was moved, as by beauty. Unthinkingly, she had clasped her hands in her lap, her hands white against the black flannel skirt; with that yoga performing flexibility of hers, that age had not ye taken from her, she had made herself compact, int a grieving ball, as if about to be shot from a can non. "I'm sorry," she was apologizing, "I don't *wan* to feel this way, I want to be cheerful and gutsy an flip about it, this is ridiculous. Even the children—

"Especially the children," he said. "They're goo sports."

"And I'm not, huh?" Joan said, in a voice a shad less hopeless, brightened by her aptitude for fai appraisal. "I am in some ways. It's just, just"—th points of skin, the tears of flesh, sharpened—" wake up every morning reciting reasons to myse why I shouldn't jump in the river. You don't kno what it's like."

She was, as always, right: he didn't. He imagine nothing, thinking of her jumping in the river, bu how cold the water would be, and how heavy he black flannel skirt would become. She was a stron smooth swimmer and the river was not deep. "We do you know what *I* felt like," he said, "lying besid you all those years waiting for something to hap pen."

"I know, I know, you've said it a thousand time I thought some things did happen, once in a whil but look, I don't want to argue. I'm not complainin about the *facts*, it's just, just—"

"Just you want to die," he finished for her.

She nodded, with a sob. "Then I think how in-ılting that is to everybody. To the children."

Studying her, admiring her compact, symmetrical ose, he wanted to die with her; he felt she was rouching at the foot of a wall that was utterly lank, and the wall was within him. He wished to e out of this, this life and health he had achieved ince leaving her, this vain and petty effort to be appy. His happiness and health seemed negligible, ompared to the consecrated unhappiness they had hared. Yet there was no way out, no way but a umb marching forward, like a soldier in a dis-redited cause, with tired mottoes to move him. You were depressed when you were living with ıe," he told Joan. That was one of the mottoes.

"I know, I know, I'm not *blam*ing you, I'm not elling you to *do* anything, just—"

"Just what?" He shifted weight. His legs were ching; he glanced at his wristwatch. He had a date keep.

"Under*stand*."

"If I understood any more," he confessed, "I'd e totally paralyzed." He asked her, "How can I elp you, short of coming back?"

"That *would*n't help, I'm not asking that."

He didn't believe this; but the possibility that it as true lifted his heart, a little greedy lift, like a sh engulfing a falling flake in an aquarium. The flake tasted bitter. "What are you asking, sweetie?" He regretted calling her "sweetie." He had tried to amalgamate and align all his betrayals but they still multiplied and branched.

"That you know what it feels like."

He said, "If I'd been better at knowing what you feel like, we might not have come to this. But we *have* come to it. Now let go. You're just tormenting everyone this way, yourself foremost. You're healthy, you have the children, money, the house, friends; you have everything you had except me. Instead of me you have a freedom and dignity you didn't have before. Tell me what I'm doing wrong," he begged.

She had to laugh at that, a little cluck; it occurred to him that her pose was a hatching one, her immobility a nesting hen's.

He was getting later. Joan knew it. He had to get out, to move on. "You have a lot of life ahead of you," he tried. "It's a *sin*, to talk about death the why you do. Why must this go on and on? I hate it. I feel glued fast. I come out here to see the children, not to have you make me feel guilty."

She looked up at last. "You feel about as guilty as a—" They waited together for what the simile would be. "Bedpost," she finished, taking the nearest thing to her, and they both had to laugh.

Here Come the Maples

They had always been a lucky couple, and it was just their luck that, as they at last decided to part, the Puritan Commonwealth in which they lived passed a no-fault amendment to its creaking, overworked body of divorce law. By its provisions a joint affidavit had to be filed. It went, "Now come Richard F. and Joan R. Maple and swear under the penalties of perjury that an irretrievable breakdown of the marriage exists." For Richard, reading a copy of the document in his Boston apartment, the wording conjured up a vision of himself and Joan breezing into a party hand in hand while a liveried doorman trumpeted their names and a snow of confetti and champagne bubbles exploded in the room. In the many years of their marriage, they had gone together to a lot of parties, and always with a touch of excitement, a little hope, a little expectation of something lucky happening.

With the affidavit were enclosed various frightening financial forms and a request for a copy of their marriage license. Though they had lived in New York and London, on islands and farms and for one summer even in a log cabin, they had been married a few subway stops from where Richard now stood, reading his mail. He had not been in the Cambridge City Hall since the morning he had been granted the license, the morning of their wedding. His parents had driven him up from the Connecticut motel where they had all spent the night, on their way from West Virginia; they had risen at six, to get there on time, and for much of the journey he had had his coat over his head, hoping to get back to sleep. He seemed in memory now a sea creature, boneless beneath the jellyfish bell of his own coat, rising helplessly along the coast as the air grew hotter and hotter. It was June, and steamy. When, toward noon, they got to Cambridge, and dragged their bodies and boxes of wedding clothes up the four flights to Joan's apartment, on Avon Street, the bride was taking a bath. Who else was in the apartment Richard could not remember; his recollection of the day was spotty—legible patches on a damp gray blotter. The day had no sky and no clouds, just a fog of shadowless sunlight enveloping the bricks on Brattle Street, and the white spires of Harvard, and the fat cars baking in the tarry streets. He was twenty-one, and Eisenhower was President, and the bride was behind the door, shouting that he mustn't come in, it would be bad luck for him to see her. Someone was in there with her, giggling and splashing. Who? Her sister? Her mother? Richard leaned against the bathroom door, and heard his parents heaving themselves up the stairs behind him, panting but still chattering, and pictured Joan as she was when in the bath, her toes pink, her neck tendrils flattened, her breasts floating and soapy and slick. Then the memory dried up, and the next blot showed her and him side by side, driving together into the shimmering noontime traffic jam of Central Square. She wore a summer dress of sun-faded cotton; he kept his eyes on the traffic, to minimize the bad luck of seeing her before the ceremony. Other couples, he thought at the time, must have arranged to have their papers in order more than two hours before the wedding. But then, no doubt, other grooms didn't travel to the ceremony with their coats over their heads like children hiding from a thunderstorm. Hand in hand, smaller than Hänsel and Gretel in his mind's eye, they ran up the long flight of stairs into a gingerbread-brown archway and disappeared.

Cambridge City Hall, in a changed world, was unchanged. The rounded Richardsonian castle, red sandstone and pink granite, loomed as a gentle giant in its crass neighborhood. Its interior was varnished oak, pale and gleaming. Richard seemed to remember receiving the license at a grated window downstairs with a brass plate, but an arrow on cardboard directed him upward. His knees trembled and his stomach churned at the enormity of what he was doing. He turned a corner. A grandmotherly woman reigned within a spacious, idle territory of green-topped desks and great ledgers in steel racks. "Could I get a c-copy of a marriage license?" he asked her.

"Year?"

"Beg pardon?"

"What is the year of the marriage license, sir?"

"1954." Enunciated, the year seemed distant as a star, yet here he was again, feeling not a minute older, and sweating in the same summer heat. Nevertheless, the lady, having taken down the names and the date, had to leave him and go to another chamber of the archives, so far away in truth was the event he wished to undo.

She returned with a limp he hadn't noticed before. The ledger she carried was three feet wide when opened, a sorcerer's tome. She turned the vast pages carefully, as if the chasm of lost life and forsaken time they represented might at a slip leap up and swallow them both. She must once have been a flaming redhead, but her hair had dulled to apricot and had stiffened to permanent curls, lifeless as dried paper. She smiled, a crimpy little smile. "Yes," she said. "Here we are."

And Richard could read, upside down, on a single long red line, Joan's maiden name and his own. Her profession was listed as "Teacher" (she had been an apprentice art teacher; he had forgotten her spattered blue smock, the clayey smell of her fingers, the way she would bicycle to work on even the coldest days) and his own, inferiorly, as "Student." And their given addresses surprised him, in being different—the foyer on Avon Street, the entryway in Lowell House, forgotten doors opening on the corridor of shared addresses that stretched from then to now. Their signatures— He could not bear to study their signatures, even upside down. At a glance, Joan's seemed firmer, and bluer. "You want one or more copies?"

"One should be enough."

As fussily as if she had not done this thousands of times before, the former redhead, smoothing the paper and repeatedly dipping her antique pen, copied the information onto a standard form.

What else survived of that wedding day? There were a few slides, Richard remembered. A cousin of Joan's had posed the main members of the wedding on the sidewalk outside the church, all gathered around a parking meter. The meter, a slim silvery representative of the municipality, occupies the place of honor in the grouping, with his narrow head and scarlet tongue. Like the meter, the groom is very thin. He blinked simultaneously with the shutter, so the suggestion of a death mask hovers about his face. The dimpled bride's pose, tense and graceful both, has something dancerlike about it, the feet pointed outward on the hot bricks; she might be about to pick up the organdie skirts of her bridal gown and vault herself into a tour jeté. The four parents, not yet transmogrified into grandparents, seem dim in the slide, half lost in the fog of light, benevolent and lumpy like the stones of the building in which Richard was shelling out the three-dollar fee for his copy, his anti-license.

Another image was captured by Richard's college roommate, who drove them to their honeymoon cottage in a seaside town an hour south of Cambridge. A croquet set had been left on the porch, and Richard, in one of those stunts he had developed to mask unease, picked up three of the balls and began to juggle. The roommate, perhaps also uneasy, snapped the moment up; the red ball hangs there forever, blurred, in the amber slant of the dying light, while the yellow and green glint in Richard's hands and his face concentrates upward in a slack-jawed ecstasy.

"I have another problem," he told the grandmotherly clerk as she shut the vast ledger and prepared to shoulder it.

"What would that be?" she asked.

"I have an affidavit that should be notarized."

"That wouldn't be my department, sir. First floor, to the left when you get off the elevator, to the right if you use the stairs. The stairs are quicker, if you ask me."

He followed her directions and found a young black woman at a steel desk bristling with gold-framed images of fidelity and solidarity and stability, of children and parents, of a somber brown boy in a brown military uniform, of a family laughing by a lakeside; there was even a photograph of a house—an ordinary little ranch house somewhere, with a green lawn. She read Richard's affidavit without comment. He suppressed his urge to beg her pardon. She asked to see his driver's license and compared its face with his. She handed him a pen and set a seal of irrevocability beside his signature. The red ball still hung in the air, somewhere in a box of slides he would never see again, and the luminous hush of the cottage when they were left alone in it still traveled, a capsule of silence, outward to the stars; but what grieved Richard more, wincing as he stepped from the brown archway into the summer glare, was a suspended detail of the wedding. In his daze, his sleepiness, in his wonder at the white creature trembling beside him at the altar, on the edge of his awareness like a rainbow in a fog, he had forgotten to seal the vows with a kiss. Joan had glanced over at him, smiling, expectant; he had smiled back, not remembering. The moment passed, and they hurried down the aisle as now he hurried, ashamed, down the City Hall stairs to the street and the tunnel of the subway.

As the subway racketed through darkness, he read about the forces of nature. A scholarly extract had come in the mail, in the same mail as the affidavit. Before he lived alone, he would have thrown it away without a second look, but now, as he slowly took on the careful habits of a Boston codger, he read every scrap he was sent, and even stooped in the alleys to pick up a muddy fragment of newspaper and scan it for a message. *Thus,* he read, *it was already known in 1935 that the natural world was governed by four kinds of force: in order of increasing strength, they are the gravitational, the weak, the electromagnetic, and the strong.* Reading, he found himself rooting for the weak forces; he identified with them. Gravitation, though negligible at the microcosmic level, *begins to predominate with objects on the order of magnitude of a hundred kilometers, like large asteroids; it holds together the moon, the earth, the solar system, the stars, clusters of stars within galaxies, and the galaxies themselves.* To Richard it was as if a faint-hearted team overpowered at the start of the game was surging to triumph in the last, macrocosmic quarter; he inwardly cheered. The subway lurched to a stop at Kendall, and he remembered how, a few days after their wedding, he and Joan took a train north through New Hampshire, to summer jobs they had contracted for, as a couple. The train, long since discontinued, had wound its way north along the busy rivers sullied by sawmills and into evergreen mountains where ski lifts stood rusting. The seats had been purple plush, and the train incessantly, gently swayed. Her arms, pale against the plush, showed a pink shadowing of sunburn. Uncertain of how to have a honeymoon, yet certain that they must create memories to last till death did them part, they had played croquet naked, in the little yard that, amid the trees, seemed an eye of grass gazing upward at the sky. She beat him, every game. *The weak force,* Richard read, *does not ap-*

preciably affect the structure of the nucleus before the decay occurs; it is like a flaw in a bell of cast metal which has no effect on the ringing of the bell until it finally causes the bell to fall into pieces.

The subway car climbed into light, to cross the Charles. Sailboats tilted on the glitter below. Across the river, Boston's smoke-colored skyscrapers hung like paralyzed fountains. The train had leaned around a bay of a lake and halted at The Weirs, a gritty summer place of ice cream dripped on asphalt, of a candy-apple scent wafted from the edge of childhood. After a wait of hours, they caught the mail boat to their island where they would work. The island was on the far side of Lake Winnipesaukee, with many other islands intervening, and many mail drops necessary. Before each docking, the boat blew its whistle—an immense noise. The Maples had sat on the prow, for the sun and scenery; once there, directly under the whistle, they felt they had to stay. The islands, the water, the mountains beyond the shore did an adagio of shifting perspectives around them and then—each time, astoundingly—the blast of the whistle would flatten their hearts and crush the landscape into a wad of noise; these blows assaulted their young marriage. He both blamed her and wished to beg her forgiveness for what neither of them could control. After each blast, the engine would be cut, the boat would sidle to a rickety dock, and from the dappled soft paths of this or that evergreen island tan children and counselors in bathing trunks and moccasins would spill forth to receive their mail, their shouts ringing strangely in the deafened ears of the newlyweds. By the time they reached their own island, the Maples were exhausted.

Quantum mechanics and relativity, taken together, are extraordinarily restrictive and they, therefore, provide us with a great logical engine. Richard returned the pamphlet to his pocket and got off at Charles. He walked across the overpass toward the hospital, to see his arthritis man. His bones ached at night. He had friends who were dying, who were dead; it no longer seemed incredible that he would follow them. The first time he had visited this hospital, it had been to court Joan. He had climbed this same ramp to the glass doors and inquired within, stammering, for the whereabouts, in this grand maze of unhealth, of the girl who had sat, with a rubber band around her ponytail, in the front row of English 162b: "The English Epic Tradition, Spenser to Tennyson." He had admired the tilt of the back of her head for three hours a week all winter. He gathered up courage to talk in exam period as, together at a library table, they were mulling over murky photostats of Blake's illustrations to *Paradise Lost*. They agreed to meet after the exam and have a beer. She didn't show. In that amphitheater of desperately thinking heads, hers was absent. And, having put *The Faerie Queene* and *The Idylls of the King* to rest together, he called her dorm and learned that Joan had been taken to the hospital. A force of nature drove him to brave the long corridors and the wrong turns and the crowd of aunts and other suitors at the foot of the bed; he found Joan in white, between white sheets, her hair loose about her shoulders and a plastic tube feeding something transparent into the underside of her arm. In later visits, he achieved the right to hold her hand, trussed though it was with splints and tapes. Platelet deficiency had been the diagnosis. The complaint had been she couldn't stop bleeding. Blushing, she told him how the doctors and internes had asked her when she had last had intercourse, and how embarrassing it had been to confess, in the face of their polite disbelief, never.

The doctor removed the blood-pressure tourniquet from Richard's arm and smiled. "Have you been under any stress lately?"

"I've been getting a divorce."

"Arthritis, as you may know, belongs to a family of complaints with a psychosomatic component."

"All I know is that I wake up at four in the morning and it's very depressing to think I'll never get over this, this pain'll be inside my shoulder for the rest of my life."

"You will. It won't."

"When?"

"When your brain stops sending out punishing signals."

Her hand, in its little cradle of healing apparatus, its warmth unresisting and noncommittal as he held it at her bedside, rested high, nearly at the level of his eyes. On the island, the beds in the log cabin set aside for them were of different heights, and though Joan tried to make them into a double bed, there was a ledge where the mattresses met which either he or she had to cross, amid a discomfort of sheets pulling loose. But the cabin was in the woods and powerful moist scents of pine and fern swept through the screens with the morning chirrup of birds and the evening rustle of animals. There was a rumor there were deer on the island; they crossed the ice in the winter and were trapped when it melted in the spring. Though no one, neither camper nor counselor, ever saw the deer, the rumor persisted that they were there.

Why then has no one ever seen a quark? As he walked along Charles Street toward his apartment, Richard vaguely remembered some such sentence, and fished in his pockets for the pamphlet on the forces of nature, and came up instead with a new prescription for painkiller, a copy of his marriage license, and the signed affidavit. *Now come . . .* The pamphlet had got folded into it. He couldn't find the sentence, and instead read, *The theory that the strong force becomes stronger as the quarks are pulled apart is somewhat speculative; but its complement, the idea that the force gets weaker as the quarks are pushed closer to each other, is better established.* Yes, he thought, that had happened. In life there are four forces: love, habit, time, and boredom. Love and habit at short range are immensely powerful, but time, lacking a minus charge, accumulates inexorably, and with its brother boredom levels all. He was dying; that made him cruel. His heart flattened in horror at what he had just done. How could he tell Joan what he had done to their marriage license? The very quarks in the telephone circuits would rebel.

In the forest, there had been a green clearing, an eye of grass, a meadow starred with microcosmic white flowers, and here one dusk the deer had come, the female slightly in advance, the male larger and darker, his rump still in shadow as his mate nosed out the day's last sun, the silhouettes of both haloed by the same light that gilded the meadow grass. A fleet of blank-faced motorcyclists roared by, a rummy waved to Richard from a laundromat doorway, a girl in a seductive halter gave him a cold eye, the light changed from red to green, and he could not remember if he needed orange juice or bread, doubly annoyed because he could not remember if they had ever really seen the deer, or if he had imagined the memory, conjured it from the longing that it be so.

"I don't remember," Joan said over the phone. "I don't think we did, we just talked about it."

"Wasn't there a kind of clearing beyond the cabin, if you followed the path?"

"We never went that way, it was too buggy."

"A stag and a doe, just as it was getting dark. Don't you remember anything?"

"No. I honestly don't, Richard. How guilty do you want me to feel?"

"Not at all, if it didn't happen. Speaking of nostalgia—"

"Yes?"

"I went up to Cambridge City Hall this afternoon and got a copy of our marriage license."

"Oh dear. How was it?"

"It wasn't bad. The place is remarkably the same. Did we get the license upstairs or downstairs?"

"Downstairs, to the left of the elevator as you go in."

"That's where I got our affidavit notarized. You'll be getting a copy soon; it's a shocking document."

"I did get it, yesterday. What was shocking about it? I thought it was funny, the way it was worded. Here we come, there we go."

"Darley, you're so tough and brave."

"I assume I must be. No?"

"Yes."

Not for the first time in these two years did he feel an eggshell thinness behind which he crouched and which Joan needed only to raise her voice to break. But she declined to break it, either out of ignorance of how thin the shell was, or because she was hatching on its other side, just as, on the other side of that bathroom door, she had been drawing near to marriage at the same rate as he, and with the same regressive impulses. "What I don't understand," she was saying, "are we both supposed to sign the same statement, or do we each sign one, or what? And which one? My lawyer keeps sending me three of everything, and some of them are in blue covers. Are these the important ones or the unimportant ones that I can keep?"

In truth, the lawyers, so adroit in their accustomed adversary world of blame, of suit and countersuit, did seem confused by the no-fault provision. On the very morning of the divorce, Richard's greeted him on the courthouse steps with the possibility that he as plaintiff might be asked to specify what in the marriage had persuaded him of its irretrievable breakdown. "But that's the whole point of no-fault," Joan interposed, "that you don't have to say anything." She had climbed the courthouse steps beside Richard; indeed, they had come in the same car, because one of their children had taken her Volvo.

The proceeding was scheduled for early in the day. Picking her up at a quarter after seven, he had found her standing barefoot on the lawn in the circle of their driveway, up to her ankles in mist and dew. She was holding her high-heeled shoes in her hand. The sight made him laugh. Opening the car door, he said, "So there *are* deer on the island!"

She was too preoccupied to make sense of his allusion. She asked him, "Do you think the judge will mind if I don't wear stockings?"

"Keep your legs behind his bench," he said. He was feeling fluttery, light-headed. He had scarcely slept, though his shoulder had not hurt, for a change. She got into the car, bringing with her her shoes and the moist smell of dawn. She had always been an early riser, and he a late one. "Thanks for doing this," she said, of the ride, adding, "I guess."

"My pleasure," Richard said. As they drove to court, discussing their cars and their children, he marveled at how light Joan had become; she sat on the side of his vision as light as a feather, her voice tickling his ear, her familiar intonations and emphases thoroughly musical and half unheard, like the patterns of a concerto that sets us to daydreaming. He no longer blamed her: that was the reason for the lightness. All those years, he had blamed her for everything—for the traffic jam in Central Square, for the blasts of noise on the mail boat, for the difference in the levels of their beds. No longer: he had set her adrift from omnipotence. He had set her free, free from fault. She was to him as Gretel to Hänsel, a kindred creature moving beside him down a path while birds behind them ate the bread crumbs.

Richard's lawyer eyed Joan lugubriously. "I understand that, Mrs. Maple," he said. "But perhaps I should have a word in private with my client."

The lawyers they had chosen were oddly different. Richard's was a big rumpled Irishman, his beige summer suit baggy and his belly straining his shirt, a melancholic and comforting father-type. Joan's was small, natty, and flip; he dressed in checks and talked from the side of his mouth, like a racing tout. Twinkling, chipper even at this sleepy hour, he emerged from behind a pillar in the marble temple of justice and led Joan away. Her head, slightly higher than his, tilted to give him her ear; she dimpled, docile. Richard wondered in amazement, Could this sort of man have been, all these years, the secret type of her desire? His own lawyer, breathing heavily, asked him, "If the judge does ask for a specific cause of the breakdown—and I don't say he will, we're all sailing uncharted waters here —what will you say?"

"I don't know," Richard said. He studied the swirl of marble, like a tiny wave breaking, between his shoe tips. "We had political differences. She used to make me go on peace marches."

"Any physical violence?"

"Not much. Not enough, maybe. You really think he'll ask this sort of thing? Is this no-fault or not?"

"No-fault is a *tabula rasa* in this state. At this point, Dick, it's what we make of it. I don't know what he'll do. We should be prepared."

"Well—aside from the politics, we didn't get along that well sexually."

The air between them thickened; with his own father, too, sex had been a painful topic. His lawyer's breathing became grievously audible. "So you'd be prepared to say there was personal and emotional incompatibility?"

It seemed profoundly untrue, but Richard nodded. "If I have to."

"Good enough." The lawyer put his big hand on Richard's arm and squeezed. His closeness, his breathiness, his air of restless urgency and forced cheer, his old-fashioned suit and the folder of papers tucked under his arm like roster sheets all came into focus: he was a coach, and Richard was about to kick the winning field goal, do the high-difficulty dive, strike out the heart of the batting order with the bases already loaded. Go.

They entered the courtroom two by two. The chamber was chaste and empty; the carved trim was painted forest green. The windows gave on an ancient river blackened by industry. Dead judges gazed down from above. The two lawyers conferred, leaving Richard and Joan to stand awkwardly apart. He made his "What now?" face at her. She made her "Beats me" face back. "Oyez, oyez," a disembodied voice chanted, and the judge hurried in, smiling, his robes swinging. He was a little sharp-featured man with a polished pink face; his face declared that he was altogether good, and would never die. He stood and nodded at them. He seated himself. The lawyers went forward to confer in whispers. Richard inertly gravitated toward Joan, the only animate object in the room that did not repel him. "It's a Daumier," she whispered, of the tableau being enacted before them. The lawyers parted. The judge beckoned. He was so clean his smile squeaked. He showed Richard a piece of paper; it was the affidavit. "Is this your signature?" he asked him.

"It is," Richard said.

"And do you believe, as this paper states, that your marriage has suffered an irretrievable breakdown?"

"I do."

The judge turned his face toward Joan. His voice softened a notch. "Is this *your* signature?"

"It is." Her voice was a healing spray, full of tiny rainbows, in the corner of Richard's eye.

"And do you believe that your marriage has suffered an irretrievable breakdown?"

A pause. She did not believe that, Richard knew. She said, "I do."

The judge smiled and wished them both good luck. The lawyers sagged with relief, and a torrent of merry legal chitchat—speculations about the future of no-fault, reminiscences of the old days of Alabama quickies—excluded the Maples. Obsolete at their own ceremony, Joan and Richard stepped back from the bench in unison and stood side by side, uncertain of how to turn, until Richard at last remembered what to do; he kissed her.